THE
PLANTER

Kathy,
Read this book
and have a
wonderful life.
Pat John

THE PLANTER

A Short Novel

By PAT JOBE

iUniverse, Inc.
Bloomington

THE PLANTER
A Short Novel

iUniverse books may be ordered through booksellers or by contacting:

iUniverse
1663 Liberty Drive
Bloomington, IN 47403
www.iuniverse.com
1-800-Authors (1-800-288-4677)

ISBN: 978-1-4759-0287-7 (sc)
ISBN: 978-1-4759-0288-4 (ebk)

Printed in the United States of America

iUniverse rev. date: 10/08/2012

To Bill Jobe, my brother who sells my books to strangers and one of the nicest guys you'll ever meet, and to his wife, Gloria, one of the nicest women you'll ever meet.

The Oracle of Delphi, Jesus, Moses, Quan Yin, the Chinese goddess of compassion, and Buddha sat for hours smiling at one another, nodding and winking.

Chapter One

C AROL TANIC FELT THE POWER of the planter first, though it would be several days before she realized what had happened. She was not broke that first day she drove on Brown Mountain Road in the foothills of North Carolina. She did owe the IRS $2,500 and paid them $85 per month, and her mother had lent her $9,000 on her home equity line, and Carol was making those payments. She did not consider herself broke. She did think a lot about money, but did not consider herself broke.

She sold advertising for Rutherford Weekly, a 36-page fish wrapper and fire starter that ran photos of local festivals and ignored murders, rapes, drug deals, car wrecks, and house fires. She did not particularly like her work, though it paid her few bills and kept food, yes even an occasional slice of chocolate cheesecake, in her belly. But it was not a work that held her heart. Her heart hungered to work in the field of spirituality.

The planter caught her eye. It sat on the deck of a blue, double-wide mobile home, just up the hill from Brown Mountain Road, a two-lane black top that lay north of Rutherfordton, the tiny foothills town where her paper was published and several generations of her ancestors lay in the city graveyard.

The planter stood three feet high, a dingy gray, festooned with ivy, really nothing out of the ordinary. Mary Crenshaw, the owner of the planter, set it at the corner of her deck nearest the road, so that she could sit on her deck, look at it, then look out at the mountains of her beloved Western North Carolina, a part of the country known for mountain vistas, primitive Christianity, conservative politics, and bluegrass music.

Although Mary Crenshaw and Carol Tanic had never met before that day, they would learn, in the passing days, that their worlds were altogether different, and yet they both nestled their dreams, their families, their ordinary lives in such a way as to see those rolling mountains and draw solace from their beauty.

The two women were born twenty years apart. Carol was born the year the United States exploded a hydrogen bomb on Bikini Atoll, the largest above ground test of a nuclear weapon in the history of the world. 1954 was also the year Puerto Rican radicals rushed the floor of the U.S. House and shot up a few congressmen before being killed by capitol police. The Korean War was over. Hank Williams died the year before. Elvis Presley exploded on the national stage.

And in just a few months, Rosa Parks would refuse to give her seat on a Montgomery bus to a white person, signaling an end to legal racial discrimination, although it would take a while longer to change the human heart.

But Carol Tanic was not thinking about changing the human heart, although she often did, when she spotted the planter on the corner of Mary Crenshaw's deck. What happened, as she would remember it, did not feel like thought at all. She just turned her car around and drove back to the Crenshaw home.

She walked across the top of the hill from the Crenshaw's driveway to the steps leading to the deck, and stopped and stared at the planter. In a newspaper interview weeks later, she said, "It did not occur to me then that anything unusual was happening. I simply stood there staring at it, as one might look at a beautiful painting hanging on the wall of an art museum or a beautiful view of the mountains."

Mary Crenshaw, who saw Carol Tanic through the storm door of her double-wide, had never seen a painting hanging on the wall of an art museum, but she loved to look at the mountains. They filled her heart.

"Billy Ray," she said to her husband of thirteen years. "There's a woman standing on our front steps staring at that new planter I bought the other day."

"Well, go see what she wants," he said not taking his eyes off the wide screen TV where Walker Texas Ranger was whipping some Middle Eastern looking bad guy into a puddle of pain.

Mary did not want to go out there. Something deep within her suspected Carol of being . . . what? She couldn't say. It did not feel threatening in the sense that Carol might be a distraction for some burglar or terrorist who was circling the house and preparing to ravage them all. In fact, it felt just the opposite to Mary. Carol, who looked ordinary and unassuming in a pair of jeans and a lavender top, a short crop of graying hair and a pair of bifocals. Carol looked like an angel or a Sunday School teacher who might be bringing the quarterlies for next Sunday's lesson. Mary did not feel threatened by her, but distracted by a sense that she might be an emissary from Jesus.

Like most daughters of the Christian South, Mary felt greeting an emissary from Jesus could be a mixed blessing.

And that feeling would turn out to be true.

"Can I help you?" Mary asked and barely cleared the door frame. She stood, as so many folks do when piqued by curiosity, open to learning the lesson of the moment in one sense and ready to yell for Billy Ray to get his gun in the other, although she was certain, at a deep level, there was nothing about Carol Tanic that would need killing or even scaring back to her car with a few warning shots.

"Is there any more ironic phrase in all the English language?" Carol asked surprising herself. She did not usually confront anybody. "Can I help you? Those words are friendly enough if we think about just the words. But when we hear them from store clerks or office gatekeepers they sound hostile. The underlying tone sounds as though we have interrupted the person who asks the question or even pricked a low grade anger."

Mary surprised herself. "Ma'am," she said to the obviously older woman, a woman who looked old enough to be her mother, "I have no idea what you're talking about." But she smiled, and in that smile, opened a door to Carol Tanic that would leave both of them wondering deeply about what changes might come to the human heart.

"What's she want, Mary?" Billy Ray called, still unmoved from his rock-a-lounger perch in front of Walker Texas Ranger.

Mary ignored her husband, which was something she never did.

"There's something about that planter," Carol said and looked back at the terracotta urn, which someone had painted that dingy gray, a decorating decision that mystified Carol, but the green ivy saved it somehow. Somehow it was beautiful. And of course, that was not all.

"I like it," Mary said, paused for a second and offered, "We home school our daughter," Mary added, and that shocked her. She wondered instantly why she had said that, but as if on cue, Lisa, 12 years old and freckled like her mama, walked onto the deck, too, and Carol smiled at the smiling freckled child that greeted her.

"Can we help you?" Billy Ray said after abandoning Walker and standing next to his wife.

"He works second," Mary explained to Carol, who she figured might wonder why her husband would be home at one in the afternoon. "Second" in the language of foothills North Carolina is shorthand for second shift, usually three to eleven in a local manufacturing plant.

"Are you a missionary?" the girl asked, and her mother would remember that, would know in that question that Lisa, too, sensed something Jesus-sent about the mousy-haired woman in glasses on their front deck.

"No, I sell advertising for Rutherford Weekly," Carol answered Lisa first, and then looked at Billy Ray, "I was just telling your wife that this planter is truly beautiful."

Billy Ray smiled a little then. For some reason all four of them just kept smiling at each other.

"I got a TV show I'm watching," he said and slipped back into the double wide.

"Well, I know this must seem a little strange," Carol said, and turned to go. "Thank you for your time. I really need to get back to work."

And that would have been enough, a few words spoken on the front porch among strangers, a footnote to an ordinary day none of the four of them would remember, except that was how it all started, not with their respective births, not with all that had gone on before they were born, not ancient history, the Civil War, the Reformation, or even the great thoughts and actions of Tolstoy, Thoreau, Gandhi, Emerson, Stanton, Anthony, or M.L. King. It did not even begin with Mary's trip to the building supply store where she was intrigued with the planter.

It all began that day with Carol Tanic's feeling that she should stop her car and walk up to that porch and look at that planter, an impulsive response to a feeling, a change of plans, or as Bob Dylan might have called it, a simple twist of fate.

When Carol got home that afternoon, she found a check in the mail for one thousand and twenty seven dollars, and a letter explaining that her car insurance company had overcharged her for premiums for the last six years, and she was due a refund.

She slumped into the desk chair in front of her computer and said, "Thank you, Jesus," which was strange, or at least a little strange, because she was an atheist.

But she was an atheist who loved Jesus. In fact, she believed everybody would love Jesus if they just didn't have to deal with Christians.

Alfred Merrimon was certainly not a Christian. He had been raised among the church-going folk of Nebraska and had risen like yeast to one of the top slice, white bread jobs in the Consistent Life and Indemnity Insurance Company of Omaha. But his spiritual energy he gave to making money, and he confined his exposure to the carpenter from Nazareth to occasional Sunday mornings among the Methodists of Main Street United Methodist Church. He never let it distract him from making money.

"You want to explain this to me?" he asked Averill Lumkin, the accountant who had brought it to his attention.

"It's pretty much computer generated," Averill, who was a Nebraska Lutheran, but still not a man who gave much thought to questions like, "What Would Jesus Do?" or the more liberal parody, "Who Would Jesus Bomb?"

"Six million, three hundred thousand, eight hundred and forty two dollars in premium refunds just goes out the door because of a screw up in a computer program?" Merrimon asked.

"It's all right there in the software, sir," Lumkin said and swallowed hard.

"And our third-quarter profits were twenty-six million?" Merrimon asked.

"Yessir," Lumkin answered.

Merrimon stared out the 34th floor of the Consistent Life Building in Omaha and took a deep breath. The Chinese have been teaching the power of deep breathing for five thousand years. Merrimon was not thinking about the Chinese or even the fact that he was breathing deeply. He had learned the technique as a stress management tactic years before and did it without thinking.

"And how many customers were affected?" Merrimon, who was the company's vice president for finance, asked.

"Over twenty six thousand, sir," Lumkin answered.

"For an average refund of?"

"Just over two hundred and forty dollars," Lumkin answered.

"Worst case scenario?"

Lumkin fell silent. He was a man used to looking at rows of figures, not dreaming up disasters, even if he were an insurance accountant.

"I'll tell you the worst case scenario," Merrimon stood from behind his desk and walked to wide windows of his Omaha office. "The stock holders notice it as a line item in the annual report and raise hell with us for making a six million dollar mistake in the way we collected those premiums."

"We didn't pay any interest on the money, sir. We just gave it back," Lumkin said.

"Excellent point, my boy," Merrimon said to the younger, lower ranking minion in the Consistent Life family. "And God knows we made a ton of interest on that money while it was in our coffers, but let's not dwell on the positives for the moment. For the moment let's stew in the juices of an irate group of stockholders who chew us out for having to give back six million dollars under any circumstances, shall we?"

Lumkin swallowed hard and felt pressure behind his eyes, but he nodded and managed to utter, "Very well, sir."

"Those are just unpleasant juices, and I can see our beloved bosses blistering our hides in the wake of that stock holders meeting, but I don't think either of us would lose our jobs after such an ass chewing. We will assure them that the software has been fixed, the books are in great shape now, and we will not be refunding any more premiums ever again. Does that sound about right to you, Lumkin?"

The younger man felt better. That sounded very good.

"Of course, sir," Lumkin said.

"Good," Merrimon returned to his desk and propped both hands on the surface, laced his fingers in a relaxed gesture. "There's one more thing I'd like you to do, Lumkin, before this report is seen by the stock holders."

"What's that, sir?"

"I'd like you to spread this six million dollars through 63 categories of costs that the company has born this quarter, so the stock holders don't even notice it."

"I beg your pardon, sir?"

"We both speak English, Lumkin. I don't need to repeat myself. Can you imagine undifferentiated write-downs for pretax catagories?"

"Sir?"

"How about capital improvements to anticipated preproduction outsourcing of overseas assets?" Merrimon spoke without cracking a smile.

Lumkin had been in accounting for Consistent Life for 18 years. He might be younger and lower ranking than Merrimon, but he was no dummy.

"Sir, we are neither an oil company, nor a Wall Street hedge fund," he began.

"Don't even start with me, Lumkin. You and I go a long way back. You know as well as I do that this company does not invest in risky investment instruments. We are not holding the paper on subprime mortgages and we have not written any policies on cruise ships off the coast of Somalia. We used a piece of software that overcharged our customers for the past 20 years, and it was only a fraction and the only people who are even aware of it are you, a few people in your department, and 26,000 people who have already spent the money at the grocery store, so I am telling you to hide this six million dollars so neither one of us loses our jobs over it. Am I making myself clear?"

Lumkin followed his logic, and answered quickly, "Very clear, sir. Clear as a bell, sir. Very clear."

Mac Hartwell owned a picture of Simone Weil, whose last name is pronounced "Vay," if you can believe that. He had taped the picture, which he had found in a head shop in San Francisco, to the mirror in his bathroom. He believed if Simone Weil could live 34 years that ended in the maelstrom of the Nazi occupation of France, he could live in post-modern America reading New Age philosophy, feeding his cat, whom he had named Mr. Friskers, and watching movies he rented in Marion, North Carolina.

Mac, like Carol Tanic and Mary Crenshaw, drew strength from the great sloping hunks of mountain that rounded every horizon in Western North Carolina. Mac had spotted fires for the N.C. Forest Service and had written for The McDowell News and had run a program for special kids in the schools in Marion and had done all kinds of stuff to pay his bills and keep his cat and belly fed.

And like Carol Tanic, he had been a babe in arms when Elvis first started to shake, and like Carol Tanic, he found himself casting about, pacing, walking in the woods, sucking strength from the mountains, nursing the milk from the great rounded teats of the Carolina hills, and like Carol Tanic, he found his mind blown by receiving a check from Consistent Life. His was only for $134, but at the time he had been out of work for a couple of weeks so $134 looked like two tanks of gas and two trips to the grocery store and two trips to the movie store. During one of those trips, he rented "Across the Universe," and sat through images inspired by the Beatles and their music.

And Mac Hartwell wondered, "What universe? Do they mean the one that holds the stars in the sky or the one that holds a trillion living cells within the confines of my body? Are they singing about swirling clouds of gas or are they singing about the capacity of the human imagination to place universes inside the atomic structures of other universes, and what about miracles and signs and fires that burn on distant hills? What about these Carolina mountains, these mounds of rock and dirt that host ferns and laurels that grow nowhere else in the world? Or do they?"

Carol Tanic and Mac Hartwell had been friends for 30 years. They had been lovers for about ten minutes once in an office they shared in Rutherfordton, when they both worked for The Rutherford Express, a 24-page fish wrapper and fire starter than published stories about life in the shadows of those mountains, a paper that carried pictures and news of car wrecks, house fires, murders, rapes, and the returns from various elections, including how the people of Rutherford County had voted for president. The majority had not backed a Democrat since Harry Truman.

That is to say that John Kennedy, Lyndon Johnson, Jimmy Carter, Bill Clinton, and Barack Obama had all become president without the majority of voters in Rutherford County, a fact that did not bother that majority in the least.

Carol and Mac had found ten minutes to be enough sex to remain friends. Carol had said to Mac once, "Friend is better. Then nobody has to leave."

He appreciated the logic without having much affection for the result. Mac liked sex, but maybe not as much as friendship. He couldn't figure why the two had to be exclusive. He wrote if off to an axiom of his: "Life is full of mysteries."

Carol called Mac on the phone.

"I had the strangest thing happen," she said. "I got a refund check from my insurance company. Apparently I had been overpaying my premium for years and they just now figured it out."

Silence.

"Mac, did you hear me?" Carol asked.

"You know how we're always noticing synchronicity and seeing it as a sign of being on the right path?" Mac asked.

"You've got to be kidding," she said and inhaled to dramatize the moment.

"Not kidding. I got a check from my insurance company, too," he said, and they both laughed.

"Wow," she oozed in the vernacular of a generation raised on The Beatles and The Rolling Stones. "What do you think it means?"

"I dunno. What do you think it means?"

"It means I'm gonna pay a little extra to the IRS, my mom's home equity line, and my dentist," she said.

"Don't spend it all on debt," he blurted. He caught himself. "Hey, it's your money, but I just feel spiritually led to say, debt is not ever going away if we give all our energy to debt."

"I know. I know. I'll probably give some to the women's shelter, too, and maybe take the captain out to eat," Carol said.

"The captain," was her nickname for her 12-year-old son, Jake Tanic, who lived with his dad in Chesnee, a South Carolina town just over the state line.

"Yes, good, treat the captain, but I worry about the spiritual energy you give to that women's shelter," Mac said.

Carol sometimes wanted to reach through the phone line and strangle Mac. Steeped in the New Age language of all kinds of star gazers and donut glazers, he usually made her feel good with his talk of "spiritual energy," but sometimes she just wanted to do what she wanted to do without his feedback.

"That women's shelter saves lives, and sometimes women feel the spiritual energy it takes to leave the men who beat them nearly to death," she said and felt the anger rising in her voice.

"Okay, we won't go there," Mac lowered his tone, as he trained himself to do when dangling his tendrils in the dangerous waters of angering others.

Carol knew him too well.

"Just because you are pissing me off doesn't mean we don't have to go there. You know that I'm a zealot when it comes to violence against women, which often means violence against their children . . ."

"I know, I know," Mac tried to cut the sermon short.

"Okay, I know you've heard it all before, but kiss my ass, buddy row. If you don't want to know what I plan to do with the money, don't ask," Carol fumed, and then added, "Sometimes loving you over the phone is a lot worse than being married to either of my ex-husbands."

"Oh," Mac yelled in feigned pain. "That knife will be hard to extract from my rib cage, but I can manage. No need to dial 911."

"Yeah, right," she soldiered on. "Just stay on the line until I can chamber a few rounds, and I'll put you in the hospital for sure."

"My dear, dear nonviolent friend," Mac chided in fun.

"As long as my gunplay is imaginary, you can handle it," she said.

"All reality begins as thought," he reminded her, and they agreed to change the subject, to move on in the conversation, to hardly notice that they had both received checks from Consistent Life. Of course, they had no way of knowing they were among more than 26,000 other customers who had also received checks totaling more than six million dollars.

Carol Tanic sold advertising. Selling advertising consists of walking into car lots, beauty salons, restaurants, real estate offices, mortuaries, tire stores, pawn shops, hardware stores, paint stores, and other small businesses and pointing at various sized boxes on printed pages and telling the business owners how much it would cost to see their business advertised in that box.

Print advertising, as it is called, dates back to the early part of the 18th century, when folks like Ben Franklin printed broadsheets that contained news, schedules of community events, predictions of the weather, editorials, gossip, and letters from readers, some of which, in Franklin's case especially, were not letters at all, but thinly veiled expressions of opinion written by Franklin who signed concocted names to the letters so that the public might think someone else held some of his more outrageous positions.

Nothing appealed to Carol Tanic more than outrageous positions. She believed the world was possessed of a collective madness that created wars, hunger, torture, rape, global warming, and other symptoms of this collective madness, which could easily be cured if people only thought like her.

And Carol suspected deeply that she was not alone. In fact, in many of her phone calls to Mac Hartwell and other friends, she would speak of her love for a utopian vision, not of a perfect world, but of a world where reasonable people saw no need for standing armies, something she considered as contributing factors to many wars, no need for poor farming practices or greedy corporate control of food supplies, something she saw as creating at least some of the hunger in the world, although she did admit war figured in there, too. She saw no need for power structures that caused one group to devalue another, a major cause of torture, no need for men to disrespect women, a major cause of rape, and saw no need for technologies that spewed carbon into the atmosphere, a precursor to global warming.

Carol saw, and often spoke of, the world as suffering in undue ways because of the simple refusal of reasonable people to see clear solutions to obvious problems.

To the world she looked like an aging ad sales lady, but in her own heart, and sometimes within the hearing of her friends, she was a zealot.

"So do you think half the rich people in the world could cure world hunger?" she asked Mac on the phone.

"I don't really think about things like that. I know you do, and I think it's lovely," Mac said to Carol.

"What about a quarter?" she asked.

"Did you notice my answer to your first question, and just decide to ignore it, or were you genuinely not interested?" he asked.

"I read once that the square root of one percent could do it, or actually I read, and I can't remember where I read it, maybe in one of Greg Braden's books, that the square root of one percent of any group can significantly affect the thinking and therefore the work of an entire group," she said.

"Really?" Mac asked, giving up hope of his half of the conversation counting for much when she gets on a roll.

"Really. That would account, I suppose, for such a small percentage of the English colonists coming up with the idea of the American Revolution, and hanging onto the will to fight it for seven years, and eventually win it, even though they lost almost every battle they fought with the British," she said.

"I'm just going to set the phone down and walk away. Scream really loudly when you want me to actually participate in this conversation," Mac said.

"Oh, don't be silly. I know you don't think about things like this, but I also know you are a dear friend, and you will let me blather on endlessly, or at least for a few minutes about my passions to end war, feed the hungry, cure most preventable diseases and put a nice school and health clinic in every village in the world," she said.

"What about bad breath?"

"Sure, let's give out universal breath mints while we're at it," she said and laughed at his joke. "You're such a dear to put up with me."

"And you are to put up with me, sweetheart," Mac called Carol, "sweetheart," in that dear Southern manner, rather than in that way that would connote his actually having an interest in her romantically.

She went back to see Mary and Billy Ray Crenshaw.

"There's something about that planter, Billy Ray," Mary said to her husband during an episode of Wheel of Fortune.

"Can you believe how good Vanna White still looks?" Billy Ray said to his wife.

"You reckon how many women around the country hear that question from their husbands on such a regular basis as to be sick unto death of hearing it?" Mary asked Billy Ray.

"I'm sorry, honey, what did you say?" Billy Ray asked Mary.

"I said the house is on fire, the dog just choked on Lisa's left tennis shoe, and Vanna White is sitting in the driveway blowing her horn and waving for you to run jump in the car with her," Mary said through clinched teeth.

"Are you okay?" Billy wondered through a mask of faked horror.

"Mama," Lisa spoke from the doorway of the TV room, "There is something about that planter. People keep stopping to look at it."

As mother and daughter walked to the front door, a young couple stepped through the yard toward the deck. The younger member of the couple, a man who looked to be in his mid-twenties with a shock of glorious black hair and a light step, looked up at Lisa and Mary and said, "We saw your planter from the road. It's really quite amazing."

"What's amazing about it?" Billy Ray's voice surprised both his wife and daughter.

"It's almost as though it's giving off some kind of vibration," the woman, maybe in her mid-thirties, a little heavier than the man, but no less enthusiastic, said of the planter.

"No, that would not be right," Billy Ray said and raised his hand as though he were directing traffic to stop. "It's not giving off any kind of vibration."

The couple, who were holding hands, laughed and brought their other hands up to their mouths. Billy Ray thought they might be drunk.

"Ya'll are acting kind of funny. Can ya'll just go on about your business?" he said and started to wave his hand like he was shewing flies.

"Billy Ray," Mary sounded startled and turned to face her husband.

"It's okay, ma'am. We didn't mean to bother you," the woman insisted and turned to pull her boyfriend away from the deck.

"Ya'll don't mind my daddy," Lisa offered with a smile. "He ain't into vibrations."

Chapter Two

BILLY RAY CRENSHAW WAS NOT a mindless extension of his television set. He worked stamping metal parts for automobile engines. He had finished high school and served a hitch in the army. He was a loyal son of the White Standard Baptist Church and had once pulled a screaming baby from a house blaze as a member of the Gilkey Volunteer Fire Department. Like others in his family, he had ordered his life to sustain minimal damage, stay sober, have a little clean fun, and die and go to heaven.

As his daughter put it very well, he ain't into vibrations.

"If anybody else comes to look at that planter, I don't want you nor Lisa talking to them," Billy Ray said.

"What makes you figure anybody else is coming to look at our planter, Billy Ray?" Mary asked with a straight face and rubbed her palms along her blue jean covered thighs.

"Well, how about the obvious fact that nearly a dozen people have already come," Billy Ray said and made it clear from his tone that he was not expecting to put up with any more visitors, or any smart-mouthed lip from his wife.

"We can't control it, Daddy. It's like the wind," Lisa said.

Billy Ray looked at his daughter as though he were seeing her for the first time. The 12-year-old freckled face had always had a seriousness and a steady gaze that belied her age or child-like enthusiasms or anything else that might be expected from a little girl. Sometimes she got on his last nerve.

She asked a lot of questions in Sunday School.

"If God loves us, why would he let anybody go to hell?" was one that got her a frown and a clucked tongue from Miss Ruth Merelyn, her Sunday School teacher. But Miss Ruth Merelyn had been honest enough to admit she just didn't know the answer to that question.

"I don't know," Miss Ruth Merelyn had said and raised her eyebrows and opened her hands and shrugged her shoulders, and said, "The Bible says it, so it must be true."

She was a bit of a bother at school, too. That's why Billy Ray and Mary had decided to take her out and home school her.

"Why do we say Columbus discovered America, when the Native Americans were already here?"

Her teacher wondered where she picked up the term, "Native Americans."

"I watch Jon Stewart on the Comedy Channel," she said.

But most disturbing to Billy Ray, and more intriguing to Mary were the few times in their lives with Lisa that she had said things like, "Why do you and Mommie just walk right through the angels like they aren't even there?"

She spent a lot of time out in the fields and hillsides behind their Brown Mountain Road home. The rocks and trees spoke to her heart like little birds and mice in a Disney movie. She felt their voices in her heart more than hearing them in her ears, and there was, for her, a music and a heart in everything. She harvested spirit fruit, and ached to see and feel that there were not others in her family, among her friends at church, among her cousins or uncles or aunts, there were not others who shared her sense of spirit in everything. She wondered why that was so.

And she figured out early on that she alone, at least as far as she could tell, she alone saw angels.

Sometimes there would only be one snoozing in her daddy's Lazy Boy Recliner when she came home from church. But other days she would step out of her bed to find her room crowded with them, attending angels like butterflies rising and falling among the furnishings of her room, some smiling and winking at her, a sign she took to say that all is well, and others talking among themselves, laughing, complimenting each other on treasured objects that sat about in Lisa's room, a crystal she had found by a mountain stream, or a wild turkey feather she had brought home from one of her hikes.

For her one of the great moments in any day was watching her mother and father at breakfast totally ignoring the one or two or 17 angels who flew in and out of their breakfast vignettes like clowns or pantomimes, juggling beams of light or standing on each other's shoulders to make Lisa smile.

"She's always so happy," Billy Ray said one morning, almost as if to say there might be something wrong with her.

"I believe it comes from a very deep place," Mary said and nodded, and looked at her smiling daughter with a knowing gaze.

And that was because Mary did know something. She wasn't exactly sure how, and sometimes she doubted it, the way all mothers do, but she felt certain that Lisa had a special commission from the universe or God or Jesus or whoever did the heavy lifting in the spirit world. She felt her daughter would likely become a spiritual teacher, certainly not a minister since they were Southern Baptists, and God knows their girls don't grow up to be ministers, or if they do, they have to turn Methodist or Presbyterian or Unitarian or something awful like that.

No, Mary was certain, at least some of the time, that Lisa would teach. In fact, she felt her daughter was teaching her husband the day she said, "We can't control it, Daddy. It's like the wind."

And Billy Ray, who was not a mindless extension of his television set, despite the hours he spent in front of it, had sense enough not to say something stupid, so he said, "What does that mean?"

"Remember in the Bible when Jesus says not to look for the kingdom of heaven over here or over there, because it is like the wind. You can't see the wind, but you know where the wind has been because the branches of the trees are moving. You can see where the wind has been, but you can't see the wind," Lisa said.

"You're very good at knowing what the Bible says," Billy Ray nodded, but the questioning look stayed on his face.

"You know what else Jesus said about the kingdom of heaven, Daddy?" Lisa asked.

"Tell me, sweetheart," he said knowing full well he would have no idea what she might say.

"He said the kingdom is within you, Daddy," she said with very little drama, just a little crinkle around her eyes and a slow and steady gaze.

"I am lost," her big daddy said. "How does that have anything to do with people stopping to look at the planter on the front porch?"

Lisa twisted her mouth to one side and sniffed, as she might have if her daddy had asked her a math question.

"You said you don't want no more people coming, but Daddy, there are some things in life you can't control, like the wind and the kingdom of heaven being within you, inside you, like a beam of light or a super power, like in a movie or something," she said.

He suddenly reddened.

"Honey, you know I love you," Billy Ray started.

"And you know I love you, too, Daddy," Lisa said.

"But, sweetheart, we just can't have a bunch of people coming up in our yard looking at that planter like it's some kind of space ship or something," Billy Ray insisted and stood, "And that's all I want to hear about it."

Lisa tucked her head, and skipped out of the room, but not until after she had said, "Okay, Daddy."

He looked over at Mary, too, and stuck a finger in the air at her, "And nothing else out of you, either."

Mary smiled and nodded and imitated her daughter's voice to say, "Okay, Daddy."

Lumkin stood before Merrimon with a computer print out in his hand.

"Yes?" the older, higher-ranking official of Consistent Life said to the younger, lower-ranking accountant.

"I took the liberty, on my own time, of course, of analyzing the numbers from that refund mailing," Lumkin said.

Merrimon looked up from his massive desk, which sat in front of his expensive art collection, which contained his high-dollar collection of alcoholic beverages, and nothing else that would offend any of the Protestants who lived around him in Omaha, Nebraska.

"What refund mailing?" Merrimon asked him after a long and studied silence.

"I understand, sir, that it is the refund mailing which shall not be named, but just between the two of us, I thought you might be fascinated, by a remarkable co-incidence," Lumkin said confidently, much as any human being exudes confidence when in possession of information that someone else doesn't know.

"Just between the two of us?" Merrimon asked.

"I can assure you, sir, I have not shared this data with my wife or my secretary or anyone else in the department, and it is not in a form that could be retrieved by a janitor or a waitress looking over my shoulder at a coffee shop," Lumkin said and smirked and his eyelids floated down as if he were presenting the Queen of Spain with a map of the Caribbean, ripe for conquest.

"Go on," Merrimon finally agreed. Lumkin placed the print out on his desk. It was nothing more than a column of five-digit numbers.

"Zip codes?" Merrimon asked.

"Yessir," Lumkin agreed.

"Zip codes that run from the twenty-two thousands up to the twenty-nine thousands?" Merrimon asked.

"Yessir," Lumkin concurred again and nodded this time.

"Am I missing something?" Merrimon asked, his voice straining with a smattering of irritation.

"These are the only zip codes the software sent the checks to, sir," Lumkin said calmly.

"My God!" Merrimon almost jumped out of his seat. "Does this mean there are hundreds of other zip codes out there just waiting for this crazy software to spit out thousands more checks?"

"Impossible, Mr. Merrimon," Lumkin opened his hand and spread it to show the bases had been covered. "That software has been replaced. It can't mail any more checks to anybody."

"Well, then what's your point? Get to it, man," Merrimon took a deep sigh through his large proboscis, and Lumkin again took on the air of one about to reveal a map to King Tut's treasures.

"Sir, as you know, we have over three million customers. Their dispersion through the general population of America and Canada is roughly the same as the population itself. We have many more customers, for instance, in New York City than we do in rural Nova Scotia, but our numbers are very close to the numbers of the general population," Lumkin began to ramble and his boss interrupted him.

"I know this, Lumkin, for God's sake, get to the point," Merrimon almost growled in frustration.

"The point is, Mr. Merrimon, that the odds of 26,000 people getting a refund from us and all living in the same western counties of three states are almost beyond calculation. None of these checks went to California or Utah or Pennsylvania. They all went to the zip codes on this print out to small, mountain communities from southern Virginia to western North

Carolina to the mountainous corner of South Carolina. None of them went anywhere else," Lumkin finished with a flurry that would have made a magician proud.

"Are you saying we sent six million dollars to a bunch of hillbillies?" Merrimon asked.

"I am, sir," Lumkin said and nodded.

"I don't guess any of them were named Jed Clampett, were they?" Merrimon asked with a smile.

"No sir, I checked," Lumkin said and returned the smile.

"Were we hacked?" Merrimon asked.

"I'm still checking," Lumkin said.

"Just between the two of us," Merrimon added and raised his right index finger for emphasis. "Just between the two of us."

Carol Tanic started writing a book. She had written a lot as a teenager, and since wandering in the wilderness of different sales and advertising jobs, she had done what she called "dabbling" in fiction, essays, articles for whatever newspaper or magazine she was working for, but this felt like a book.

In the days following her visit to the planter and receiving the check from Consistent Life, two incidents she had not related to each other or to her writing, she had begun writing a book called, "The Jesus Of My Imagination."

She has also dreamed some intense dreams. In fact, the first line of her new book read, "I have begun dreaming intense dreams, dreams about Jesus. In one such dream, I have been told, as if I were alone in a giant sports arena and a voice came over the speaker system. The voice said, 'Preach the Gospel.' I don't feel that I have any choice about that."

Within hours of dreaming that dream and beginning that book, she spoke on the phone with a friend who lived in a nearby city. They chatted about the ordinary glories and gores of their lives. Just as the conversation was winding down, Carol said, "I dreamed I am supposed to preach the Gospel of Jesus Christ, so would you mind if I preached some Gospel to you right now?"

Silence on the other end of the line did not surprise Carol, but her friend quickly recovered, and said, "Oh, sure, go ahead." Her friend, after all, professes a faith that gets into her a local church on a regular basis, so why not hear the Gospel preached over the telephone?

"This is the Gospel of Jesus Christ as I find it in the very fiber of my being. You are fine just the way you are. You are an object of so much love that you deserve everything wonderful you ever dreamed of. The best walks in the rain, the best conversations around campfires, the best dancing and singing, the best sex, the best food, the best, the very, very best you ever dreamed of. In fact, the best you ever dreamed of is just a fraction of what you deserve because the whole universe is a conspiracy of love and joy and peace and freedom and humor, all of which is in your favor, designed to celebrate you and all whom you love and all they love until at last we come to a full awareness that William Blake was right, all that lives is holy."

More silence loomed on the other end of the phone line. Even more silence vibrated in the ears of the two people, Carol on one end and her friend on the other end. Her friend began to laugh and moan with pleasure and ooze soft sounds of "Oh," and "Oh, my," and finally she said with a light in her voice that had not been there before, "I don't believe my preacher has been reading the same Bible you have been reading."

Carol told that story in her book. She typed that story into her computer screen, and looked back at it, and sighed with pleasure, and said to herself, "I believe that would be right."

The war in Iraq had ground five years out of the moral currency of many Americans. Some, like Carol Tanic and Mac Hartwell, became so depressed at the thought of it that they could barely speak. There had been several marches against the war in Asheville, which is the largest city in the mountains of North Carolina, and Carol had even ridden on a bus to Washington to march against the war with 250,000 other citizens of the United States, to say that they did not want their money or their neighbors or their flag or their government killing people in another country to secure our oil supply, to exact revenge for President Bush's father and the war he had won in 1991, but also the war a lot of people said he should have finished by taking out Sadam Hussein.

Carol and Mac and other people who could remember Vietnam and Cambodia and Laos and other misadventures of American foreign policy felt a deep and inconsolable sadness at every thought of the U.S. invasion of Iraq, especially the children who had died in the fighting, the four million refugees, the 600,000 civilian dead, the generations of Iraqis who would feel the pain of war in the very cells of their guts, and yes, the thousands of Americans, military and civilian, dead, and the tens of thousands, military and civilian impaired for life by the loss of eyes and arms and legs and wholeness shattered by the blood and the steel and the cries in the night.

The war had disheartened them so that it affected their work, their marriages, the way they raised their children, how they looked at the sky and the ground and the rivers and the sea. It cooled their coffee and warmed their beer, kept them awake at night and made them sleepy in the middle of the day. It darkened their light and lighted their darkest dreams with bizarre and horrible thoughts as liquid as, "It it's okay for the government to kill people, why isn't it okay for me to do it, or at least hate somebody who has more than me or whose skin is a different color or who plays his music too loud at red lights or maybe even cheat on my wife or girlfriend or husband or boyfriend or cheat on my taxes or cheat my business partner? What difference does it make if we can assemble the most powerful military in the history of the world and spend a billion dollars a week to kill people who have done nothing to us and inspire them to kill each other? What difference does it make?"

Billy Ray and Mary Crenshaw looked across their living room at each other. Lisa slept in her bed all cozy and warm. W. Dixon Franklin sat on the sofa next to Mary.

He had a Jimmy Carter grin.

"I've traveled all over the world and spoken with religious leaders from many nations. I've taught the Bible on television for over 30 years. I can assure you, this is a miracle," he said and nodded and kept grinning like Jimmy Carter.

In the yard outside their home, fifteen people stood staring at the planter.

"Can't we just donate it to some church?" Billy Ray asked.

"Most miracles are considered linked cosmically to the spot on which they take place," W. Dixon said and shook his head and looked off into a corner of the room as if he were searching deeply implanted computer files. "I think this will run its course in a few years, and when it does, you folks might be able to return to a normal life."

"How about we just move and leave the planter here?" Billy Ray asked.

"I think that would be a decision we would have to make as a family," Mary said.

Billy Ray felt like somebody had just hit him. He had that just-been-smacked-by-somebody-totally-unexpected feeling in his chest and belly and just about everywhere he could feel anything. A decision we would have to make as a family? She was contradicting him in front of a stranger?

W. Dixon paid no attention to the tension in the room, and continued to talk. In 30 years of Bible teaching and church house preaching, he had developed a reputation for continuing to talk.

"Your family's presence here may be critical to the manifestation of the miracle," W. Dixon said. "It may be that the Holy Spirit is using all of you to speak to all of us of his will and his power."

"This is completely crazy," Billy Ray held up his hand and shook his head. "Preacher, I got all kinds of respect for you and your television show and all, but this is just too weird for me to take in."

"I understand, son. I really do. Imagine how the disciples must have felt when the Risen Lord showed up in the Upper Room," W. Dixon said.

"You think this is like that?" Billy Ray asked.

"No, but I think it is most certainly a miracle of God," the old TV preacher answered.

Just around the corner, down the hallways from where they sat talking, Lisa had climbed out of bed and was sitting in the floor, her blanket rapped around her, nodding her head and smiling to herself.

Carol Tanic caught her breath when she read the first story in The Daily Courier, the local paper of record for Rutherfordton, the town where she lived and sold ads for the competition paper, a paper that was not a paper of record but rather what is called in the business, a shopper, a printed fish wrapper or fire starter with the sole purpose of selling stuff.

Carol often mused to herself that since its sole purpose was to sell stuff, the paper, in fact, had no soul.

The other paper, on the other hand, The Daily Courier, did have soul. It had the soul that all small town papers have, the soul to report the news, the house fires, the murders, the rapes, the drug deals, the drug deals gone bad that that end up in murders and rapes, the deaths and births, the weddings and funerals, the ebb and flow of a community's life, and the politics and religion, letters to the editor that scream of the madness in the life of the letter writer who believes there is so much madness in the life of those opposed, that the writer fails to notice the madness in his or her own life.

Carol sometimes wondered if she missed the madness in her own life, but not this day. This day she was highly distracted because a local reporter had written a story about the planter on the Crenshaws' front deck, a planter, according to the story that had drawn dozens of visitors to stop by the Crenshaw home and stare at the planter.

Carol was riveted by the story, of course, because she remembered quite clearly, because she, too, had been drawn to the rather ordinary looking planter and had found it somehow captivating. At the time, Carol did not know she had been first, but she would learn that soon enough.

She felt riveted, captivated as soon as she realized that she, too, had been on Brown Mountain Road and had stopped and stared at the planter and found it beautiful. But she nearly jumped out of her skin when she read well into the story that Abigail Whisnant of nearby Polkville, North Carolina, had gotten in her car for no reason and driven to Rutherfordton, a trip of about twenty miles and guided by nothing other than an inner sense that she needed to go there, had driven straight to the Crenshaw home and exited her car and stared at the planter.

Coincidentally, that same day, she had received a check from the Consistent Life Insurance Company, a refund for more than a thousand dollars in overpaid premiums.

Carol's hand shook as she reached for the telephone to call Mac Hartwell.

"We have not been hacked, sir," Lumkin reported back to Merrimon.

"You'd bet your retirement on it?" Merrimon asked.

The younger, lower ranking man hesitated. Swearing by his mother's grave didn't feel like a lot to ask. Offering up a body part felt to him like a reasonable standard by which to measure his certainty, but betting his retirement felt like quite a pledge. Still he had checked and double-checked. Clearly the software was written in such a way as to overcharge

26,000 customers six million dollars over a period of time.

"Then clearly the engineer who wrote the software is the source of the mistake, and he has some kind of affinity for hillbillies. Find him and have him shot," Merrimon said matter-of-factly and turned back to a report on his desk.

Lumkin froze in his position standing next to Merrimon's desk.

"I'm joking, Lumkin," Merrimon said. "Find him and turn him over to the authorities. For all we know, those 26,000 people are all cousins of his."

"I'm on it, sir," Lumkin said and shot out of Merrimon's office before the boss changed his mind and asked him to shoot somebody else.

The people of the Appalachian mountains have a reputation for being clannish, which is to say they keep to themselves, don't set their sites very high, take care of their own, will do anything in the world for you, and don't have much interest in change. Nothing too fancy for them, they pretty much like things as they are.

Yet to hint that they are all the same would be a gross miscarriage. Some have been law-abiding, Bible believing, hard working and tax paying all their lives. Others have distilled illegal spirits, grown marijuana, fished, hunted, and sold Christmas trees out of the auditing notice of the Internal Revenue Service. Many are educated and bear up under the weight of that responsibility, but many others dropped out of school early and have what they call a healthy suspicion of book learning. Many are peaceful and neighborly, but others have a violent streak that has given the region a reputation of murder and rape and drug deals and the murders and rapes that all that can bring.

Most love their children, but some beat their children to death.

Pat Taylor, a former Lt. Governor of North Carolina, said the problem with running for office in his state is that half the voters want to have prayer breakfast with you and the other half want to stay up all night drinking.

There among some of the most beautiful mountains in the world live all kinds of people: geniuses and dullards, dreamers and the imminently practical, some of whom are so level-headed that if they chew snuff it runs out of both sides of their mouths at the same time.

A high percentage attend church, and of those, there are some who believe in miracles.

"When you and I were talking the other day, Mac, you said you had gotten a refund check from Consistent Life?" Carol asked over the telephone line.

"Yes, and each of us remarked on the coincidence of our both receiving one the same day," Mac remembered. "Why do you ask?"

"Well, a woman in Polkville also got one about the same time," Carol said.

"How interesting," Mac effused, "And may I be so forward as to ask how in blue blazes you came upon this information?"

"I read in the dad gum newspaper," Carol said hardly able to contain her shaking and hoping it didn't make its way into her voice.

"How even more interesting," Mac reacted with genuine surprise, "And what interest did the newspaper have in this woman's refund check?"

"Well, this is the most interesting part of all."

And she told Mac about the planter.

"Oh my," Mac reacted. "Let me process this for just a moment." He did. They enjoyed a little silence over the phone. Mac looked out the window of his mountain cabin and watched his cat bat a dust angel. "Both you and this woman from Polkville stopped to look at this planter, admire it, interact with the people who own it on the same day that you received refund checks from the same insurance company?"

"Yes," Carol agreed.

"It's uncanny," Mac said.

"And other people are reporting a miraculous sense of well-being who stop and stare at this planter. They talk about energy, a surge of energy, an up tick in their joy. There's even a TV preacher who's started hanging out there and talking with the people who have been coming," Carol reported.

"Lord," Mac groaned. "Count on the TV preachers to swarm at any opportunity. Did any of the other people report getting checks from Consistent Life?"

"The story doesn't mention it," Carol said.

The story didn't have to mention it. The telephone started ringing on the desk of Jenifer Davis, the reporter who had written the story, within hours of the papers hitting the street.

Sixteen people who had visited the planter had also gotten checks from Consistent life. At least, sixteen people who had visited the planter and gotten checks called Jenifer Davis.

Like so many reporters who worked for The Daily Courier, Jenifer Davis had been recruited from the school of journalism at Chapel Hill, North Carolina to write for the paper for a couple of years and after that move on so she could make more money.

She had grown up in Albemarle, like Rutherfordton, a small Southern town, but east of Rutherfordton, on flatter land where there had been more textile mills and furniture plants, still a small town, just not a mountain town.

She had grown up in the Southern Baptist Church, a huge institution in the rural South. The Southern Baptist Church is so big that she once heard relatives from opposite sides of the family meeting for the first time. One woman had asked another, "Are you Southern Baptist?"

The other had replied, "Isn't everybody?"

The religious affiliations of the South include Jews, Hindus, Muslims, Buddhists, atheists, agnostics, Jains, pagans, druids, poor white trash, drug dealers, murderers, rapists, Ku Kluxers, Methodists, Episcopalians, African Methodist Episcopalians, Presbyterians, Pentecostals, Roman Catholics, members of Holiness churches, Assemblies of God, Churches of God (there are several,) nondenominational independents, Free Will Baptists, independent Baptists, and a goodly number of people who worship the Great God Almighty Dollar, but the Southern Baptists outnumber them all combined.

To say that they influence Southern culture is a little like saying sunshine influences agriculture. They are not omnipotent, as is evidenced by the fact that they can't always use the ballot box to keep beer and wine sales out of their local grocery stores or restaurants, but when Jimmy Carter, a Southern Baptist Sunday

School teacher ran for president he was elected with the electoral votes of every state in the South except for Virginia. Even the Virginians probably regret their screwing up that year after Carter's many successes in the White House.

Jenifer Davis was of that clan. She grew up straight-laced and feeling a certain confidence about that life that comes of knowing your people run things. Her daddy worked for Amalgamated Textiles in Albemarle until the plant closed and worked retraining textile workers at the local community college. Her mother taught school, served on the local library board, and fought the sale of beer and wine in local grocery stores and restaurants.

She knew several Bible verses by heart and could recite them. She believed beyond the shadow of any doubt that a carpenter from Nazareth had been killed on a cross 2,000 years ago to save her from her roasting eternally in a deep-fat fryer of hellfire and damnation, and one of the reasons she became a journalist was to apply the standards of objectivity to the critical issues of contemporary life and prove to her own personal satisfaction that her Southern Baptist upbringing was correct.

She would have gone into the ministry, but the Southern Baptists prefer male plumbing for their ministers and expect their women folk to harvest other fields.

So when her telephone began ringing like a repentant drunk at a summer revival meeting, she had a nagging suspicion she might in the midst of a miracle.

"Ma'am, this is very strange, but you are saying you got one of those refund checks from Consistent Life as well?" Jenifer asked the 16th caller.

"Yes, and I just want you to know that my husband and I have for years given to the Christian Children's Fund. You know that charity on TV that shows that pictures of pitiful little children?"

"Yes, ma'am, I am familiar with the Christian Children's Fund," Jenifer said slowly, flipping back through her notebook to look at other charities that had benefited from the accounting error of Consistent Life.

"Well, I just wanted people who read your story to know that we had given half that money to feed little children in Honduras," the woman said.

Jenifer talked with the woman a little bit more, thanked her, and hung up. She walked into her editor's office, plopped in the chair across from her, and said, "I think this is a very big story."

Carol Tanic and Mac Hartwell drove to Polkville from Mac's cabin in the woods where he hung out with his cat. Carol had found Abigail Whisnant after only a few phone calls and had made an appointment to see her after work on a Tuesday afternoon.

On the way up Mac had argued that Carol was off on a tangent, the whole trip felt like a waste of time to him, what did she really expect to come of all this, wouldn't she do better to seek some spiritual centering around the whole thing?

"You and I have spent our whole lives trying to get spiritually centered," Carol grumbled. "Sometimes I just want to do something."

Mac scratched his right eye and ran his fingers through his long blond curls. With the right mustache, beard, and blood lust, he would have looked like General George Armstrong Custer.

"It just feels like flying off the handle a little here. I love you, and you know that, and you know I say anything I have to say only in the truest spirit of love . . ."

"But," Carol interrupted, "this feels to you like I'm flying off the handle."

"I'm not saying that."

"You just did," Carol said, which caused Mac to smile and look down at the floorboard of Carol's 1995 Honda Civic.

He laughed a little.

"I really do love you."

"Oh my God, Mac, don't you get it? I love you, too. You have taught me to consult the I Ching and pray out of the Native American tradition. You've convinced me to do deep breathing, and open myself to the Yin and Yang of any situation, but something extremely weird is going on here, and it's tied up with that damn planter and these people and this money, and Jesus, Mac, can't we just sit down and talk with the woman and see what comes of it? Do we have to process the hell out of everything before we ever do anything for crying out loud?"

Mac rode along in silence. He hated how he felt in that moment. A lifetime of feeling like the weirdest person in the room came home to roost. His chest ached with the sense of being squeezed by a giant hand, or a crowd of hands, the hands of all the people who had ever wanted him just to shut up and quit processing the hell out of everything.

And Carol could tell she had bugged him badly, maybe even hurt him deeply.

"Mac, I'm sorry,"

"No," Mac held his hand up and set his jaw. "You don't get to be sorry right now. Right now, I will process the hell out of this within myself, and if you don't mind I'd like you to be quiet while I do it."

She did.

Mac was a brilliant singer, songwriter, guitarist who had spent years in a fire tower run by the North Carolina Forest Service, watching for forest fires, instead of banging on the doors of every coffee house between New York and Nashville hoping to make a living, or God help us, become a star on the popular music scene. He had been married twice, both times to women who also sang, played the guitar, loved to perform in public, and that musical part of those marriages had been a part of why both those marriages had failed.

Mac loved to explain things. He loved to tell long involved stories between songs, sometimes about the songs he was about to sing, but other times stories that clarified where he was coming from as a human being. He had come, in the last few years, to realize people really didn't care where he was coming from as a human being, and in that moment, there in the car with Carol driving to see Abigail Whisnant, he realized that maybe Carol didn't care where he was coming from as a human being, and that hurt his feelings and that made him ask Carol to be quiet.

So they rode in silence.

Carol hated riding in silence.

She felt in a fight it was the most unfair weapon. She once had a husband who she had begged to talk to her about the way he was treating their daughter.

The husband had walked out of the room, maybe embarrassed because he had felt such love for his daughter that he had made so clear to Carol that his relationship with his daughter was more important to him that his relationship with Carol. And Carol just wanted to talk about it. She wanted to understand it. She wanted to say what she wanted to say to be heard, not to be relegated to the back seat of their car for trips they would take when the daughter wanted to sit in the front seat and wanted Carol to be quiet and sit in the back and let her visit with her dad.

And all Carol had wanted was to talk about it, so she followed her husband out onto the porch of their home.

"Leave me alone!" he had screamed at her, but this time she was feeling brave, because she believed this time might be the time that she could get him to hear her, how it hurt when their daughter sat in the front seat of the car and talked to her dad and didn't want Carol to say anything, but he was furious and he didn't want to talk about it, and out on the porch of their home, he picked up a chair and threw it into the yard, and picked up another chair and shook it at Carol, and screamed, "If you don't shut up and leave me alone, what do you think I'm gonna do with this chair?"

And again she had been quiet.

She hated being quiet.

Carol Tanic was a woman eaten up with dreams. One of her dreams was that the world would change so that no one would ever again make anyone else be quiet. But she also knew it was hard for people to listen when they didn't want to listen.

Chapter Three

RUSSELL CAMBRY KNOCKED ON THE door of the Crenshaw home on Brown Mountain Road. Only about six people sat in the yard staring at the planter. Billy Ray had ordered another load of gravel for the driveway and had made it a little wider to handle a couple of extra cars.

W. Dixon sat on the deck next to the planter where occasionally he would answer a question from one of the onlookers about the Bible. Russell looked over at W. Dixon and said, "Good morning."

W. Dixon grinned his Jimmy Carter grin and answered, "Good morning."

W. Dixon had taken to spending about two hours a day at the Crenshaw home talking with the onlookers, but the Crenshaws had so far barred him from bringing a television crew and taping a segment of his show from their deck.

"Mary, I'm Russell Cambry. I'd like to offer you and Billy Ray some money to help defray the cost of having so many people visit your home," he said with a deep voice and no Southern accent, sounding like maybe he was from Florida or Ohio.

Mary had a peace about her. She and Billy Ray had prayed for God's guidance and help and maybe this man was here to bring help. The family had just finished breakfast and Lisa was working on her lessons in the kitchen. Billy Ray had hoped to get in some television, but that was becoming more difficult as the people kept coming to stare at the planter.

"Tell him to come on in," Billy Ray said from the living room and stood to shake Russell's hand.

"Thank you, Billy Ray. I guess it's been very disruptive to your lives to have this planter on your deck," Russell said after he had settled in on the sofa next to Mary. Lisa listened from the kitchen.

"Ya think?" Billy Ray snapped, and immediately was sorry as Mary caught his eye and frowned at this rudeness. "I'm sorry," he mumbled.

"Who wouldn't understand?" Russell asked hoping to smooth the feathers.

"Well obviously about two or three hundred people in the last week or so," Billy Ray blurted, but another thought jumped into his mind. "You're not another reporter are you?"

"No," Russell said, shook his head, and glanced back and forth between Mary and Billy Ray.

"Thank God for that. We didn't ask for this, mister. And I'll just tell you, although my wife and daughter don't share my feelings on this, I'd be just as happy if the whole thing went away. We had a very normal life before all this."

Russell wanted desperately to ask Billy Ray if he honestly thinks anybody lives a normal life, but he imagined the Crenshaws had things pretty orderly before all this happened. In fact, as he looked around the Crenshaw living room, he was struck by the order, the lack of clutter, the neatness, the lack of video game controllers and stacks of old mail, the few knickknacks or tacky junk store memorabilia. One of those English Jesus pictures hung on one wall and the wide screen TV sat like a black altar against another wall. A trio of family pictures hung by the door, and the lamps and side tables could have adorned any other of a hundred million living rooms across America. The room held no bookshelves, no books. The family's one copy of the New International Version of the Holy Bible lay on a small shelf next to the kitchen table, but Russell Cambry couldn't see it. The Sunday School materials were also kept there, along with coupons that came in the mail. The family did not subscribe to The Daily Courier, but feared they might have to if the paper kept writing about their planter.

"I've been very fortunate in my life. I made a great deal of money about twenty years ago, and have been on something of a spiritual journey since. There is clearly something remarkable going on around that planter," Russell said.

"We're starting to pick up on that," Billy Ray grumbled.

"Billy Ray, please," Mary barely said, but she said it.

"Will you excuse us just a minute?" Billy Ray asked Russell, but didn't really wait for an answer. He stood, stormed into the kitchen, and ordered Mary to follow, by saying, "I need to speak to you."

Their backyard was their meeting place. Lisa looked up as her mother walked calmly out the back door her father had just exited. The backyard sloped up into those beautiful North Carolina mountains. High flying clouds stood watch over the couple who were caught in this simple twist of fate.

"Since when did you start calling me down in front of company?" Billy Ray asked.

"About the time you started speaking to people so rudely," Mary answered calmly, but her arms crossed in front of her showed she was bracing for the worst.

"You are not the head of this household."

"I would not be true to the principles we both believe in if I let you speak harshly to guests in our home."

Billy Ray stepped away, twirled to one side almost like a football player trying to avoid a tackle. How could this be happening? He and Mary had been a perfect couple, not without conflict, but conflict that had always been resolved. They had always worked things out. Suddenly he felt his world coming apart.

"That TV preacher said this could go on for years," Billy Ray complained in frustration.

"If it is God's will . . ." Mary started, but Billy Ray interrupted.

"Don't you understand, Mary?" he almost whined. His voice rose and quivered. "Mary, Mary honey, I'm a volunteer fireman and a deacon in the Baptist Church. I ain't no saint or miracle worker or nothing like that," Billy Ray balled up his fists and cut through the air like an invisible boxer threatened him.

"Billy Ray Crenshaw, I love you so much," Mary matched his emotions and that caught his attention. "I've felt my heart fill with love at the sight of you for 13 years of marriage, and two years of courting before that. I would die for you if I had to, but you've got to understand something very, very important about whatever is happening to us."

He had softened listening to her talk about him. His fingers hung at his sides and he stepped closer to her, lowered his voice.

"What's that, sweet Mary?" he asked.

She scooped his hands up into hers and smiled and took a long breath.

"This is not about you. You let this thing play itself out, and maybe a lot of good will come of it. I can't say for sure, but I know it's not about you or me either one. It might have something to do with Lisa, but it's not about you and me. We've always heard the preacher say that we're just here to serve the Lord, well maybe that is what this is about. Maybe not, but I don't think our talking rudely to people is any way to serve the Lord, and I know you don't think so either."

That sounded right to him. He nodded.

Back inside Russell told them, "I'm a Buddhist. You folks might not want to work with me because of that."

Although Billy Ray could scarcely believe he did it, he turned to look at Mary, clearly signaling that she could deal with this question.

"Tell us about that," Mary said and crossed her legs and dropped her laced fingers over her knees.

Russell did. He talked about his leaving the Methodist church when he was a very young man, because of his being treated badly by some of the folks in the church. He came to realize that everybody is responsible for their own actions, and he came to believe he had participated as a victim in the bullying and mistreatment, and that there is a wholeness and balance to all of life, which had convinced him that he needed to empty himself of all expectations, fears, anxiety, to reach a point of Zen mastery where he could stand to be slapped in the face with a board by a monk in Japan and not react with anger or fear.

"But it did hurt," Lisa said from the kitchen doorway, as Russell finished his story.

"Oh yes, it hurt," Russell agreed, stood and came over to introduce himself to Lisa.

They shook hands and she asked him, "Do you ever see angels, Mr. Cambry?"

And that changed everything for Russell Cambry, a multi-millionaire who had manufactured toilet fixtures, a world traveler who was married to a devoted wife whom he also considered his dear friend and business partner, a man who "had everything" in the vernacular of the rural South, but still had a spiritual hunger that until that moment he believed had been satisfied by his strict Buddhist faith and his Zen practices. In that moment, he found a new treasure in the field of his life, took a new step, walked a new walk. In that moment he said something to Lisa Crenshaw he had never said to anyone before.

"Once or twice, maybe three times, I have seen an angel," he said.

"I never don't see them, Mr. Cambry. They're everywhere. There are four of them in this room right now, and all of them are perfectly delighted you're here," Lisa said.

Russell Cambry had tears in his eyes.

Billy Ray gestured as though he were about to speak, but Mary put her finger to her lips to keep him from saying anything. Russell looked around the room, and back at Lisa and realized he was still holding her hand from the earlier handshake.

His voice quaked with emotion.

"Will you tell them for me how happy I am that they are here?" he asked the little girl.

"Why don't you tell them yourself?" she asked.

He shook his head, but she opened her hand and gestured around the room. He looked around, saw nothing out of the ordinary, but kept looking and suddenly closed his eyes. He laughed a little, and spoke softly, "I'm very happy you're here."

The silence in the car between Carol and Mac couldn't last.

"Honey," Mac said after the passage of maybe seven or eight minutes.

"Who you calling honey?" she spoke and sniffed and laughed a little.

"I wish I could tell you," Mac began, but she interrupted.

"You can always, always tell me anything, my dear, dear friend, and in case it is not abundantly clear, let me make it very, very clear, you can take all the time you need to tell me whatever you want to tell me," Carol said.

So he did. For the next 15 minutes he talked about how much it had hurt him when people didn't listen to him, some stories Carol had heard before, which prompted him to interrupt himself and say, "You may have heard some of this before," which would prompt her to make a circular motion with her finger to indicate he should keep talking.

And as they approached Polkville, Mac could feel his story telling and explaining winding down, and he apologized.

"I'm sure there are things you want to say to me," he said.

"No need to apologize, Mac," she said. "We have the ride home for that."

Abigail Whisnant did not tell very many people about being on the Edmund Pettis Bridge in Selma with Martin Luther King, about tear gas and dogs and police officers mounted on horses and the gashes in people's heads.

She had been 23 years old that day, and as Carol Tanic and Mac Hartwell pulled into her driveway, she stared out through eyes that were 68 years old, eyes that she hoped would never again see anything like that day in Selma.

She taught history for 30 years in the Cleveland County schools and found only the most rare student who shared her passion for stories of people overcoming incredible odds. Among her favorites were Thoreau and Emerson, Tolstoy and his influence on Gandhi, who subsequently had inspired Dr. King. She talked about Seneca Falls where abolitionists gathered to begin the battle for women's rights. She told her classes, sometimes with so much emotion they sat watching her wide-eyed that Susan B. Anthony, Elisabeth Cady Stanton, and Lucy Bloomer, plus thousands more had all died of old age before finally in 1920 women had gained the right to vote. And voting mattered, she told classes filled with students, many of whom came from homes where their parents didn't vote, their grandparents didn't vote, and all the people they knew had a disdain for politics and politicians and all that represented in the exchange of power in their lives. Taxes were a curse, and government was always getting in the way, not helping things to get better.

"Miz Whisnant," as her students called her, would rail against such thinking as if she were a revival preacher.

"Politics elects sheriffs and local officials who not only have the power of arrest, but can build roads and schools, decide where hospitals and nursing homes will be placed, take all the commonly held assets of any community and apply them to books or baseball or sometimes pure tomfoolery, but if you don't vote and pay attention to elections, you have no say in who those people are and the decisions they make," she said on more than one occasion.

One student had dared to offer, "My daddy says it don't matter who the president is because there ain't no difference between the Democrats and Republicans."

Miz Whisnant stood for a minute and worked her ample mouth as though she might be hooking popcorn from between her teeth.

"I respect you father, because he is your father, and we are taught to respect our fathers and mothers," she began, "but I tell you what difference it makes who the president is. The president can get our country into war, and the president can get us out. Nothing on God's great earth is as heart-breaking and horrible as war, and before you vote to elect a president, you get down on your knees and pray with all your heart that you elect somebody with enough humility and heart of compassion to handle a job like that."

She welcomed Carol and Mac into her home with a big smile, and tumblers sweating from iced tea. She had cut slices of pound cake on plates and set them in front of her visitors as they sat around her dining room table.

Carol asked her to talk about herself.

"Not much to tell. I taught school for 30 years and loved it, volunteer in my church, don't smoke or chew and run with boys who do," she said and laughed.

"You grew up here?" Carol asked.

"On a tenant farm. Mama took in wash and cooked pies to make a little spending money. Her mama had begged her to stay in school, and she did love to read, preached education to us kids. I have a brother who was a principal and a sister who made a nurse. Both my parents were the grandchildren of slaves. We still go to family reunions with hundreds of descendants of slaves," she said and paused. "Maybe some of your ancestors owned some of mine," she said with the most gracious smile.

Mac coughed and shook his head wildly, but Carol didn't hesitate.

"My ancestors owned slaves, but, of course, the family myth is that we were good to ours," Carol said and waited for Miz Whisnant to respond.

She laughed deeply and easily.

"I understand if you meet Germans today, all their ancestors fought on the Russian front and none were members of the Nazi party," she offered.

"Yes, something like that," Carol agreed.

She cleared away the cake plates and returned to the table.

"You told me on the phone why you are here," Miz Whisnant said. "So, where do we go from here?"

"I don't know that there is anywhere to go," Mac offered.

The two women looked at him as if they expected him to say more, but he thought better of it.

"There is a part of me that is deeply suspicious of going anywhere, too," Miz Whisnant said.

Carol sat looking at her.

"Tell us more about that," she asked the retired teacher.

"At first blush, it feels like a call from God," she began. "But I remember how godly have been all the great causes of history, and some of the not so great causes. Probably no general in all of history prayed more than Stonewall Jackson, and he was on the wrong side fighting against the tide of history instead of with it and ended up being accidentally killed by one of his own men. I have a hard time seeing God in that, especially since his troops fought so well and won so many battles."

She paused and drummed her fingers on the dining room table. She looked again at the faces of Carol and Mac, the one the mousy haired ad seller, the other the blonde and handsome singer songwriter.

"So if it isn't a call from God, what is it?" Carol asked.

The older woman pulled her glasses from her nose and rubbed her hands deeply into her face. She shook her head.

"Hard to say, but I know nothing comes easy, nothing good anyway," she mused.

"What in the name of God are the two of you talking about?" Mac exploded.

"The planter," Carol answered as though it was the most obvious thing imaginable.

"What about the planter?" Mac asked.

Carol looked at Miz Whisnant. She hoped the older woman could answer Mac's question.

"This is the crux of the question," Miz Whisnant spoke as if every word had weight and depth. "What about the planter?" she repeated Mac's words. "We are in such a hurry these days to finish one task so we can move to another, to get to work so we can leave. I can't believe white people can do church in an hour. How is that possible?"

She looked at her two white guests before each of them realized they were expected to answer her last question.

Mac laughed. "I don't attend church, but when I did, I don't remember feeling that it didn't last long enough." He laughed again in hopes the two women would get his joke.

"I'm a Unitarian. Our church is a little different," Carol said.

"Yes, a little different," Miz Whisnant agreed and nodded again.

Russell Cambry, the Buddhist who had just met Lisa, the girl who sees angels, walked around the Crenshaw's land with Billy Ray.

"You have six acres?" Russell confirmed. Billy Ray nodded, and watched Russell as if he might pull a snake from his jacket at any moment. "The increase in traffic hasn't bothered your neighbors yet?"

"We can only see the folks across the road, and they haven't said anything about it," Billy Ray answered.

Russell sensed there was more to be said.

"Who are those people across the road?" Russell asked.

"Hemphills, Frank and Clarice. His daddy had a dairy farm down the road, but that was years ago. There's only a handful of dairy farms left around here.

Frank works at a garden store in town. Clarice has some kind of mail order candy business or something," Billy Ray said.

Russell waited. He had learned during years of business transactions that listening is at least as important, if not far more important than talking.

"They're Methodists," Billy Ray added.

"You don't see much of them?" Russell asked.

"Around here, if you don't go to church with people or go to work with them, you don't see much of them," Billy Ray said.

Russell felt like his curiosity had been satisfied and started walking back toward the house. "Let's go see what you and your wife think of my ideas."

When Jenifer Davis's second story ran in The Daily Courier, most people didn't have much of a reaction. A few commented on it to their friends and neighbors. Like a lot of newspaper stories, it drew some attention.

But the editor for the Associated Press in Raleigh, the state capital, took note of it. He read that 16 people had been drawn to stare at a large planter on the porch of a mountain home near Rutherfordton, and those same 16 people had received refund checks from Consistent Life. That was certainly enough of a curiosity to get it transmitted, along with other regional stories, on the wire.

The story ran the next day in regional papers, a few of which served the western mountains of Virginia, Asheville and the mountain counties of North Carolina, and the mountainous corner of South Carolina.

Some of those newspapers were read by people who received refund checks from Consistent Life.

The software engineer's name was Rudy Dudley. Lumkin learned from the software division that Dudley had left several years earlier and had moved to Thailand. That's all the information they had.

Lumkin called the State Department for information on how to contact the U.S. Embassy in Thailand.

Miz Whisnant offered to prepare supper for the trio, but Carol and Mac insisted on taking her out. Folks in Polkville eat at Aunt Sally's. In fact, back when Aunt Sally was still among the living, Elvis Presley had stopped in for a cheeseburger on a trip from Charlotte to Asheville. That caused something of a stir.

Not much stirred the night Mac pulled out the chair and held it for Miz Whisnant, the night she ordered baked ham and green beans and cornbread, Mac ordered the stew beef and a house salad and cornbread, and Carol ordered a chef salad without the meat.

"I'm a vegetarian," Carol explained.

"And a Unitarian. Just don't tell me you've been abducted by aliens," Miz Whisnant insisted.

"Oh, that would be me," Mac quipped.

"He's kidding," Carol said.

"I know," Miz Whisnant agreed and laughed.

While they waited for their food, Mac grinned broadly and gestured with an open hand to invite more information.

"I don't think I'm being paranoid here, but it feels to me as though the two of you know something I don't know," he talked as though to sound light hearted, but he did reveal a little concern.

"He hasn't see the planter yet," Carol offered.

"Well, that explains it," Miz Whisnant said.

"Explains what?" Mac insisted.

For some reason that tickled Carol and Miz Whisnant no end, and they both laughed loud enough to draw a few glances from other tables.

"And why is that funny?" Mac asked.

"Mac, we are living through a miraculous outpouring of something nobody has been able to explain to anybody's satisfaction yet. I understand there is a TV preacher on the premises down there in Rutherfordton, but my guess is he knows little more than the rest of us. As I said earlier, we are too much in a hurry these days. A little patience is required in such circumstances," Miz Whisnant spoke formally with the high tones of a school teacher, but Mac felt just as confused as ever.

"So we've driven over here to meet you, eat your delightful pound cake, and have dinner together so that you can tell us to be patient? But riding over here Carol was quite adamant that the time has come for action. What action? What is she talking about, and why won't the two of you be more clear with me about what this planter means to you and what it has to do with that insurance money?" Mac asked.

"Mac, let me tell you two things that may help clear up what is so obviously confusing to you," Miz Whisnant began. "Politics is the art of compromise, yet it has delivered into our lives certain reforms about which there could be no compromise. Does that strike you as ironic or self-contradictory in any way?"

"Can you give me an example?" he asked.

"Of course, sweetheart, I'm a school teacher, and unless they've got a bell in this place that might make me let you out of class at some arbitrary hour, I could keep you here all night giving examples," she said.

"One would suffice for now," he said and grinned.

"Women winning the right to vote," she said. "Nothing was more clearly a violation of basic human rights in its day than keeping women from voting, keeping married women from owning property, not allowing women to testify against their husbands. When the campaign began, women were so clearly legally second-class citizens that they faced an insurmountable political battle. There was no room for compromise, no gray area over which there could be some give and take, women were either going to be written into the Constitution or not. And it took nearly 80 years to come to pass. There is still broad-based discrimination against women, sexism, less pay; you name it. I will probably die before women attain full equality with men if it ever comes to pass in this land of the free and home of the brave. But I still support women candidates for public office, buy my insurance from a woman, use a woman attorney, dentist and doctor, and do anything else I can think of to support women at every level of society. Dr. King said the arc of history is long, but it bends toward justice."

"Great, wonderful, I'm not sure where this is going, but I'm along for the ride," Mac said and dug into his stew beef when the waitress put it down.

"Sounds like Miz Whisnant is still changing the world," the waitress, a former student said as she served the rest of the meal.

"With my dying breath, honey. With my dying breath," she said and started cutting her baked ham.

"You said you had two things to tell me," Mac prompted her.

"Yes, and this will seem as esoteric as a hornet in a honey comb, but stick with me," she began buttering her cornbread. "I play a game of Solitaire on the computer called Free Cell. Have you ever seen it?"

"I don't own a computer," Mac said.

"He's a Luddite," Carol interjected.

"Takes all kinds to make a world," Miz Whisnant said and signaled for the two of them to eat. "My supper's gonna be fine. You two eat while I talk. This free cell game is almost impossible to lose, unlike most solitaire games. The kind you play in Las Vegas for instance is almost impossible to win, but in this game, especially as it is played on the computer, you get to start over each time you hit a wall. The computer will even tell you at certain points in the game, 'There are no more legal plays, would you like to play again?' and it redeals the cards in exactly the same pattern. Sometimes I have played the game 20 or 30 times before I finally figure out how to arrange all the cards so that I win the game. Are you with me so far?" she asked and took a bite of her supper.

"I can see that playing this game and the women working for 80 years to get the vote are alike in that you just don't give up," Carol responded.

"Yes but," Mac raised a finger, determined to ever be the devil's advocate. "There are failures, too, right?

I mean many of the women who worked for the vote died before the right was won."

"That certainly didn't make them failures, any more than my dying will make me a failure if I am unsatisfied with the rights of women on my death bed," Miz Whisnant insisted.

"Okay, but I hear in your two illustrations an intimation that maybe every problem can be solved," Mac offered as he kept shoveling in the stew beef.

"Then you misunderstand me," she replied. "I don't believe every problem can be solved, but I believe there are universal human rights. I find evidence of them everywhere, even in human emotions like love and hate. We are a race, a human race of people who almost universally love love and hate hate. I know there are exceptions, and our most recent history is a bloody trail from Rwanda to the Sudan to Cambodia and of course, Hitler's Germany to only name the worst examples. But I'm just as starry eyed as Anne Frank on her way to her death. I believe people are basically good and that goodness will win in the end."

"The righteousness of the Lord will be revealed to all nations," Carol said.

"My Lord, a Unitarian who can quote scripture," Miz Whisnant feigned astonishment.

"And chew gum at the same time," Carol joked and winked at the old school teacher.

"I'm not sure. My reading of the I Ching teaches me that we prosper or succeed or change for the better if we allow our higher nature to rule, but it feels to me as though we live in a world where that isn't happening all that much," Mac said.

"We can always find examples of both," Miz Whisnant agreed.

A silence fell in among them, as they chewed their supper and looked around at each other and the other customers in Aunt Sally's. Mac waited, watched, swallowed a big bite and sipped on his coffee.

Carol and Miz Whisnant looked at each other.

Mac was uncharacteristically quiet. A man who loved questions and answers, he found himself intrigued with whatever was happening between these two women. Where were they headed? And why was he along for the ride?

Chapter Four

RUSSELL CAMBRY HAD ASKED MARY and Billy Ray to sit with him around their kitchen table. Lisa moved to the living room to read and eavesdrop.

"I'm prepared to spend a hundred thousand dollars to help you," he said, and glanced up for only an instant to make sure they had both heard him. "I'd like to pay off all your debts, which I hope won't take all of that hundred thousand, but if they do, there's more where that came from. I'm not the richest man in the world, but I have plenty, and this is a very important planter you have out there on your porch."

"Wait, wait," Billy Ray sucked in a long breath. "Wait, wait, wait," he began to look from Russell to his wife and back. "Hold on, please, I'm sorry. Mary,

I don't want to be rude, but this just doesn't seem right to me. A man walks into our home, meets our daughter, talks about seeing angels, walks around the land with me for a few minutes and offers to pay us a hundred thousand dollars. Mary, please, forgive me if I act a little bit stressed or excited or something, but this here is just about the most incredible thing I have ever lived through in my life, and I'm having a little trouble catching on. Can you understand that?"

"I understand it," Russell said.

"I am not talking to you, and dear God, Mary, please forgive me if that sounded rude," Billy Ray slapped his open hand against the tabletop and begged his wife for understanding. She grinned at him in her most reassuring way.

"I understand, too, Billy Ray. I'm sure Mr. Cambry is willing to take his time about whatever he has come here to do, and I'm delighted that he understands how both of us might be a bit unsettled by his offer of a hundred thousand dollars."

"So you're a bit unsettled, too?" Billy Ray could barely choke out the words.

"Yes, honey, take a deep breath," Mary urged.

"Oh, yes, deep breaths are very good," Russell seconded the motion.

Billy Ray snorted.

"No, no," Russell offered. "Deep breathing is much deeper than that," and Russell demonstrated pulling a long breath through his nose and pushing his diaphragm out so that his belly expanded like the Buddha's.

"Mister, you are a guest in my home," Billy Ray started to snap, but looked again at Mary, who had that don't-be-rude look on her face.

"Try one his way," she suggested and nodded.

Billy Ray felt that feeling he had felt earlier that his wife had grown an extra head or her body had been taken over by an alien, but he did try one Russell's way, and was amazed at how the tension in his body shifted.

Mary had been doing some shifting herself.

And she knew it was about the planter.

In the days since Carol Tanic had stopped and admired the planter, Mary had taken to visiting it at night, just before bed. Wearing her thick red terry cloth bathrobe, she had snuggled down into the porch chair that W. Dixon used in the daytime and sat and sipped on herbal tea and looked at the planter. She loved it, not the planter, but the feeling that came of looking at it. It made her feel content, and she had struggled with contentment in the years she and Billy Ray had been married. As she dared think back on the months leading up to their marriage, it was Billy Ray who had urged her to get pregnant right away, and it had not been her idea, not been her idea to stay home with the baby, not been her idea to home school Lisa. She had not argued with any of those decisions. It was not her nature to argue with either her parents growing up or Billy Ray once they had married, but she had liked her years between high school and marriage, years she had spent doing office work for the Department of Transportation, where she had clowned around with the guys in the shop, flirted with the younger ones and let the older ones tell her how awful the younger ones were. As she remembered it, she loved being young and single and pretty to practically every man who passed her by.

The planter had given her the freedom to remember all that, but how? How did it work to simply sit for a few minutes at the end of the day and stare at a big clay pot with ivy growing out of it? How did that make her feel free and easy and happy about life?

And why did she not mind sharing it with the people who wandered into her yard?

"Okay," Billy Ray said after trying a deep breath Russell's way. "That is a different kind of breathing. I see that."

"How about one more?" Russell asked.

Billy Ray took one more, deep and extending his diaphragm. He smiled.

"That is definitely different," Billy Ray said.

"The Chinese have been teaching it for 5,000 years," Russell said.

"I don't much care for the Chinese. They've taken a lot of our jobs," Billy Ray said.

"Maybe if we learn to breathe deeply enough, we can create new jobs to replace the old ones, maybe even jobs we like better," Russell said.

Billy Ray wasn't so sure about that.

"So why do you want to give us a hundred thousand dollars?" Billy Ray asked with much of the tension gone from his voice. Mary was amazed. She made a mental note to herself. Urge Billy Ray to do more deep breathing.

"This thing feels to me like it is going to get much bigger, more people, more traffic, and I think you are going to need to make a few changes around here to manage everything," Russell spoke in slow, measured words, but Billy Ray felt the tension rise again.

"You see, Mary?" Billy Ray snapped.

"Maybe another deep breath?" she suggested.

"I ain't taking no more deep breaths right now," he said and set his mouth like he might want to bite something.

"Did you not like those first deep breaths?" Russell asked.

Billy Ray thought about snapping and snarling, but he remembered that Mary wanted him to play nice, be polite, act right.

He took another deep breath.

"Imagine for a moment that more people are coming and how that will feel to you," Russell suggested.

"It feels like a dad blame carnival side show," Billy Ray said without thinking.

"And how would it feel to not think that thought?" Russell asked.

"What?" Billy Ray asked.

"Who would you be if you just sat right there in your kitchen chair across from your wife. whom you clearly love very much. and didn't think the thought that having a lot more people in your yard would be like a carnival side show?" Russell asked.

"I'd be me."

"And who are you?"

Billy Ray took another deep breath. Mary was amazed. He took one without being asked.

"I'm Billy Ray Crenshaw from Brown Mountain Road," Billy Ray said and smiled. Mary was beginning to think Russell might be a magician.

"How else would you describe yourself?"

"Her husband and Lisa's daddy."

"Anything else?"

"I run a stamping machine, volunteer with the fire department, and go to the White Standard Southern Baptist Church right here on Brown Mountain Road."

"Good, all nice stuff. Plenty to be proud of."

"Glad you approve," Billy Ray said and narrowed his eyes a little.

"Does all that feel good to you?"

"I don't see what you're driving at."

"You pretty much like your life, your family, your job, your church and fire department?"

"Of course."

"Do you think of yourself as a good man?" Russell asked.

"None is good but God, but I'm certainly not a bad guy. I don't do anything to hurt anybody," Billy Ray answered.

"Does anything change? Is your life any different when you think about your front yard as a carnival side show?" Russell asked.

"Well, of course, everything changes. That's the whole dad gum point, mister," Billy Ray frowned as if to say, "Am I the only one who gets this?"

"Everything changes in your yard as you think that thought, but nothing changes about who you are," Russell continued. "You're still Billy Ray Crenshaw, a loving husband and father, a hard worker at the plant, a good Baptist and fire fighter. In fact, if you weren't thinking that thought, you would still be exactly the nice guy that you just described: kind, caring, even peaceful."

"Peaceful is what goes missing when these crazy people come and stare at that planter on the deck," Billy Ray insisted.

"They aren't crazy," Mary interjected.

"How do you know?" Billy Ray asked without raising his voice. In fact, he asked the question and took another deep breath. Mary took one, too. His celebrated a new sense of emotional stability. Hers celebrated his.

"They just come and stare and go away. What's crazy about that? They don't scream or fall to their knees or cry or do anything that would bother the neighbors," Mary said.

"But if more come, if there's more cars, Russell is saying he thinks that's what's gonna happen for pity's sake," Billy Ray almost begged.

"Will it change who you are?" Mary picked up the thread of Russell's questions.

"It might," Billy Ray spoke in a very low voice, and glanced between Russell and his wife of thirteen years, "and I'm scared it has already changed who you are."

Dinner at Aunt Sally's was winding down. They had opted out of dessert remembering with pleasure Miz Whisnant's pound cake.

"What's next?" Carol asked Miz Whisnant as they stood in line to pay the bill.

"I want to meet some of the others," the older woman spoke quietly, and took the bill out of Carol's hand.

"This is my treat," Carol argued.

"Honey, I wouldn't hurt your feelings for the world, and it is so kind of you to offer. But take what you were gonna spend on supper and start saving for a car. That 1995 Honda is not gonna run forever," she said and winked at Carol and grinned.

On the way home, Mac asked, "What did she mean she wants to meet some of the others?"

Carol shook her head and laughed.

"I don't guess you'd be up for an extra hour of driving?" she asked with a light in her eyes and a lilt in her voice.

"Under normal circumstances I would be ready to settle in for the night, but I'm guessing you want me to see the planter," he said with a slight tone of resignation.

Jenifer Davis was frustrated that neither her story in The Daily Courier nor the wire story that ran the next day generated much attention. It felt to her as if the news consuming public had shrugged in the face of 16 people staring at the planter and receiving refund checks from Consistent Life. She had asked her editor for another shot, but the older, more experienced woman had encouraged her to move on to other stories, let this one lie for a while.

Jenifer could not. A curiosity and a strange sense of the wonder of the whole thing got her piling back into her car and driving back to Brown Mountain Road, despite the fact that the sun had already set. The sky hosted a full moon that soaked the landscape. Jenifer took it as an omen, although her Baptist upbringing would have had her call it a sign, not an omen. Omens are a little ominous for Baptists. Signs are much clearer.

"Yes, Billy Ray, I am changing in the presence of the planter," Mary said.

"I was afraid of that," her husband said.

"Should I leave the two of you to discuss this?" Russell, who had already stayed hours longer than he had planned, started to rise.

Billy Ray had called in sick. With a hundred thousand dollars on the table, he was thinking about calling in rich.

"No, Mr. Cambry, you've brought us this far. You may as well stay," Billy Ray sounded like he was holding back a low, slow burn.

"What's to be afraid of sweetheart? We're living through a miracle. How could it be anything else?" Mary asked.

"It could be of the devil," Billy Ray expressed his worst fear.

That caused Mary to drop her arms onto the tabletop and blow out a long sigh.

"Just for the record, I don't believe in a literal devil," Russell said.

"You don't believe in Jesus either if you're a dad gum Buddhist," Billy Ray groused, and Mary tipped her head and widened her eyes to beg more courtesy from her husband. Billy Ray added, "Sorry if that sounded rude."

"It was a little edgy," Russell admitted.

"Well, I sure do believe in the devil, and I ain't sure this ain't Satanic from stem to stern," Billy Ray grumbled.

"If you don't believe in a literal devil, Mr. Cambry, what kind of devil do you believe in?" Lisa asked from the kitchen doorway.

"Well I guess I believe in the devil as a figure of speech, like how someone might have the devil in his eye, and I certainly believe in deviled eggs," Russell said with a smile.

Mary and Billy Ray watched in amazement as their daughter, who often amazed them, talked with the millionaire Buddhist who had been in and out of their home and all over their land all day long.

"I believe in a literal devil who haunts the spirit world with demonic minions, but I believe their power is highly overrated and they really can't do any of us much harm as long as we keep the fruit of the spirit of love, like peace and joy and faithfulness and longsuffering, as long as we keep that fruit alive and living within us," Lisa said.

Russell too was amazed at this little girl, this freckled faced, auburn haired beauty with a big grin and a soft voice. He did, however. wonder if she ever farted or stumped her toe.

"And do you think the planter has been placed here by the Devil or one of his demonic minions?" Russell asked.

"No, of course not," she said and grinned. "My daddy is just one of those people who loves the Lord, but doesn't want him showing up at the foot of his bed telling him he has to become a missionary to Africa."

"Hey, little girl," Billy Ray started to scold, but Mary jumped in.

"Well, how about it, Mr. Deacon of the White Standard Southern Baptist Church? How would you feel if the Lord showed up at the foot of your bed and told you to become a missionary to Africa?" Mary asked with a big grin on her face.

"I'd do it," Billy Ray said and grinned back, "But I wouldn't like it," he admitted and all four of them laughed. "I wouldn't like it any more than I like that dad gum planter sitting out there on our deck drawing all kinds of people into our yard."

With that, the gravel crunched in the driveway and not one, but two cars killed their headlights, and deposited three visitors in the yard: Jenifer Davis, Carol Tanic, and Mac Hartwell.

Jenifer introduced herself quickly and recognized Carol.

"You sell ads for our competition. What's your interest in the planter?" she asked.

"Could I hold off answering that until my friend here has had a chance to see the subject of so much interest?" Carol asked and gestured across the yard to the front deck of the double-wide.

Jenifer agreed and the three of them took the short walk.

Silence, a full moon, beautiful mountains sloping all around them, and there on the front corner of the deck, a tall, gray planter sat hosting vines of ivy that spilled over the edges.

"Oh my," Mac said. He just stood there, tall, Norse, his long blond locks cascading, his sharp handsome face softened by the moonlight, his eyes steady as holes in a mask. "Oh, my," he repeated.

"What do you see?" Jenifer asked.

"Well, I'm not sure I want to be quoted in the newspaper."

"Off the record, what do you see?"

"It isn't a sight. It's a feeling. I can't help but feel very peaceful, very serene, very centered and grounded. Oh my goodness, it's almost as though I'm rooted to the center of the earth and that part of me is flowing upward to that gorgeous moon," he effused.

Carol said nothing, but the feeling was much more powerful than it had been a few days ago, and Mac was describing it exactly as she was experiencing it, deep vibrational energy, powerful, a sense of almost unheard of well-being, better, more powerful than she had ever been in her life, almost as though she were able to leap tall buildings in a single bound.

"She's the first one who came," Mary said after stepping onto the deck with her family and Russell Cambry. "That lady right there who sells ads for that little Rutherford Weekly. She was the first one who came and said there was something about the planter."

Jenifer Davis paid attention to that, and although a great many other things would occur that would be worthy of attention, somehow Jenifer knew this was important. She wrote in her notebook, "Carol T. was the first."

"Well," Mac uttered upon hearing that his dear friend had been the first.

"What was it like when you first saw it?" Russell Cambry, the big millionaire Buddhist asked from his place among the members of the Crenshaw family.

Carol so badly wanted to shrug it off, to make no big deal of it. Fifty-five years had taught her that often in life the things we think are big deals are not and the things we think are not often are.

But she did not shrug it off.

"It was incredible. I didn't say so then, but maybe I should have," Carol said as she again stared at the planter and felt its power.

"People just do what they do," Lisa piped in from where she stood in front of Russell Cambry and between her parents.

"What does that mean?" Billy Ray asked his daughter, in a quiet voice, almost as though the two of them were alone on the deck.

"People say 'should' too much, Daddy. Some people think they should lose weight or quit smoking or make more money or stop taking drugs, but people just do what they do. 'Should' is mostly a waste of time," Lisa said.

"You are a very wise little girl," Mac observed and followed his observation with a soft laugh, as if he could hardly believe he had stumbled into this wonderland.

Jenifer Davis could hardly believe it either. She knew in her gut she was covering the story of a lifetime, even if it had barely caused a ripple among the newspaper reading public. She knew something amazing was afoot.

Lumkin landed in Thailand with enough luggage to keep him going for a couple of weeks. Mr. Merrimon had cleared his calendar and basically told him not to come home without the scalp of Rudy Dudley. The scalp part was a joke, but he definitely wanted the man who wrote that software to pay. If Rudy Dudley did have 26,000 relatives in the Appalachian Mountains, he had pulled off quite a scam. If not, Merrimon felt he needed to never write software again, and he figured sufficient prison time would assure that.

Lumkin checked into a downtown Bangkok hotel, and looked out on the thousands of walkers, bicycles, motorcycles, and cars that clogged the ancient city. How, in the name of all that was holy, did Merrimon expect him to find one man in a country of millions?

His first stop at the U.S. Embassy yielded little. Yes Dudley had traveled to Thailand on a tourist visa, had applied for a work visa, and like many Americans on Thai soil, had disappeared into the lush countryside. The embassy had neither resources nor interest in tracking them down, and the locals enjoyed the benefits of having an American live among them, especially one who didn't cause trouble.

Lumkin next stopped at the Bangkok office of the Associated Press. Maybe Rudy Dudley had made the news some time in his years in Thailand.

At first, the young reporter who helped him came up with blanks on his computer searches, but he narrowed his search by eliminating the Rudy and only searching by Dudley.

Four years ago a noodle shop owner in Lampoo province claimed his business had been prospered by a special blessing from the local Buddhist temple zhao, a man named Kruba Krisida. The noodle man gave great credit to the zhao for helping him move his business from near failure to wild success and many noodle shops around the province.

The story went into great detail about an amulet the zhao had blessed for the noodle shop owner, but down in about the sixth paragraph, the noodle shop owner, whose name was Phrao Phat, said he also owed a great deal to his Canadian partner, a man named Dudley Dumpling.

The reporter, who was also an American, told Lumkin, "Sounds like a made-up name to me.

"But he's Canadian," Lumkin protested.

"Many Americans claim to be Canadian in this part of the world. The U.S. government is not very popular.

With four million refugees having lost their homes in Iraq, U.S. policy there is pretty much seen as the blunder of a lifetime."

Lumkin, who cared nothing for politics, simply stared at the reporter.

"Might be your man," the reporter shrugged.

"And where is this Buddhist zhao or the noodle shop owner?" Lumkin asked.

"Well the zhao might be on a college tour in the U.S. and the noodle guy could be anywhere in Lampoo province, but the dateline on the story is a village called Wat San Phra Chao Dang. You might start there," the reporter suggested. "It's about 200 kilometers inland. I'd hire a jeep and a driver if I were you."

"Not much to go on," Lumkin looked down at notes he'd been taking.

"You're looking for a mighty small fish in a mighty big pond, mister. I'd start where I can."

Billy Ray Crenshaw sat with his face in his hands. In a matter of days, a life he had believed would take him from the cradle to the grave had disappeared. He and Mary had agreed to take Russell Cambry's hundred thousand dollars. Mary and Russell had convinced him to bring in even more gravel and create more parking in the front yard, but people had started parking on the side of the road.

The daily crowds were growing and he knew it would only get worse. Russell had dragged a food trailer in and hired a small crew to start serving meals. Billy Ray and Mary were receiving a cut of that, and since Russell felt even more expenses were bound to arise, he agreed another hundred thousand would likely be needed.

"Billy Ray, this beats anything I have ever heard of," Mr. Withrow, his company's personnel manager told the young father sitting in front of him with his face in his hands.

"I know, Mr. Withrow, and I'm real sorry. You folks have been very good to me," Billy Ray said.

"You've been an excellent employee, son. Why don't you take a few days off to think about this, and make your decision next week, after you've had some time to smoke it over. This seems very rash to me to just up and quit after all these years," Mr. Withrow said.

"Sir, another week to think about it ain't gonna change nothing. Me and Mary has run the numbers. This man has already given us a hundred thousand dollars, and said he's pretty sure we're gonna need another hundred. We've never had much debt, but this pays off everybody we owe and leaves us with enough to live on for the next five or six years. If he gives us another hundred thousand, we can be comfortable for the rest of our lives."

"What if Lisa wants to go to college?" Mr. Withrow asked.

"He says he'll pay for that, too," Billy Ray stated and shrugged as if to ask, "What else can I do?"

Driving home from the plant that head-in-hands feeling did not leave him. What was he going to do? Mary and Lisa seemed perfectly happy to sit on the deck and visit with all these crazy people who were showing up to stare at that dad gum planter, but Billy Ray was a man of his routine, a little work, a little church, a little TV and he was happy. There was no need to complicate his life with all this, but need or not, his life had become as complicated as anything he could imagine.

But wait. Hadn't Mary argued that there were no complications, that the people in the yard were very polite and not crazy at all, although it seem crazy to Billy Ray to stare at a planter. Billy Ray would much rather stare at a television screen.

Jenifer Davis got a phone call that caught her undivided attention. Twelve of the 16 people who had visited the planter and received refund checks from Consistent Life had agreed to meet at a local restaurant and talk about their experiences. The meeting was to be chaired by Abigail Whisnant, the retired school teacher from Polkville.

Among the 12 was Carol Tanic, but not Mac Hartwell. Mac had simply said, "You're more the meeting type," but Carol had argued.

"Mac, dammit, even after the way your heart felt after seeing the planter, you aren't the least bit curious about what it all means?" Carol begged.

"I think it means we can do anything we want with our lives, our fortunes, and our sacred honor," he said paraphrasing the Declaration of Independence.

"Nice," Carol acknowledged his literary allusion, but soldiered on, "So you just don't want to do whatever you want in co-operation with other people, who have come to the same conclusion."

"I'm still seeking a centered place from which to deal with all this," Mac said.

So Carol went without him.

The meeting impressed her. An organic farmer and horse breeder joined two other retired teachers and a local heart specialist. A loan officer for a local bank sat down to dinner with them, as did a cab driver, a man who owned his cab and not much else. Three college students, and a guy who ran the truck driving school at the community college finished out the roster that included Carol and Miz Whisnant.

They talked quietly among themselves until the meal was finished. They sat around a private dining table in the back of the restaurant. They had drunk sweet tea, coffee, sodas, and water with lemon. No alcohol was served in the joint.

Miz Whisnant sat at the head of the table.

"I see one other black face here," she began. "Mr. Dart, I understand you own your taxi and make your living driving local trips." Dart nodded, smiled broadly and added a Southern, "Yes, ma'am."

"I believe Miz Hernandez has ancestry south of the border," she said and gestured toward the college girl on the other end of the table, who smiled and nodded.

"The rest of you white folks are indicative of the local power structure. America may soon be a majority nation of color, but the hills of North Carolina are still run by white folks. I don't resent it, but facts are facts. We have four men among us, which means we women folk outnumber the men two to one, and I'd say, based on my experience, that increases our odds of getting things done."

Soft laughter ticked around the room. It felt easy, although they shared a common sense of the extraordinary circumstances that had brought them together.

"Who wants to start?" Miz Whisnant asked, and they looked from face to face.

More laughter, this time a little nervous.

"Start what?" Carol Tanic asked.

"Well," Miz Whisnant intoned that deep sound that some Southern black folk use to encourage their preachers on Sunday mornings. "We know how we came together. We have all been to the planter and seen how it can touch our hearts. I guess somebody has to start in suggesting what we do now."

An awkward silence fell in among them, and their laughter was replaced by shy smiling backward and forward, in and out among their 12 faces. At last, Carol spoke again.

"My friend Mac Hartwell, who also received a check and who also has seen the planter, says we don't have to do anything. He is a great student of much New Age thinking and has read the I Ching to guide so many of his steps in life. He is a beautiful man and I love him dearly. I consider him one of my dearest friends, but I believe he is wrong. I believe whatever bizarre circumstances are at work among us are calling us to action."

"Me, too," one of the college students said.

Others nodded their heads around the room.

But again the silence, followed by the soft laughter rolled around the table.

Miz Whisnant watched and waited. She had run many a meeting in her school and church life, but she had never been to one like this. Most people want to get the meeting over with, so they can go home. Miz Whisnant sometimes wondered what was so special about home. She liked her home, her dog, her books, her easy chair, but she knew many of her acquaintances went home to that infernal television, to sit like zombies in front of a machine that created a kind of waking sleep, a plug-in drug somebody called it, a way to escape life and feel nothing before escaping even more deeply into the body's best escape, the wonderland of sleep.

But these 11 people who had joined her were so different, not anxious to end the meeting, but rather present and engaged with each other's eyes and spirits, enjoying each other's presence as much as eager to move on to the next agenda item. For this meeting, there was no agenda, no call to order, no secretary elected to take minutes. Twelve people had simply agreed to meet and have dinner because they had been to the planter and received checks from Consistent Life.

And while they sounded prepared to act together, they felt no urgency to name the action they would take. As Miz Whisnant watched them and waited, they looked at each other the way teenagers do when they are in love. She felt that kind of love in her heart. She felt enraptured, and she realized that for no good reason she loved those 11 people as much as she had loved anybody in her life. It made no sense, but it felt great.

Lumkin loved no one as he bumped along the back roads of Thailand looking for Rudy Dudley. He hated the heat, ignored the natural beauty, and seethed at the bumps in the road. He feared the Associated Press reporter had given him a bad lead in recommending he look for Dudley Dumpling, the Canadian who had partnered with the noodle merchant, but he had nothing else to go on. The disappeared software engineer left no trail in the U.S. that led anywhere else but Thailand. Lumkin could find no relatives, nothing that would offer him up.

Merrimon insisted he not contact law enforcement, but rather find Rudy Dudley first. Merrimon hoped the matter could be handled quietly, but Lumkin knew it would be tough to keep quiet a crime that involved six million dollars and 26,000 co-conspirators. He had his assignment. He was on the trail, but he hated every minute of it.

"For Pete's sake," he groused to himself. "I'm an accountant."

He felt a thickness over his skin from the sweat. He swatted the mosquitoes. He paid no attention to the magnificent mountains into which his jeep driver took him.

Chapter Five

HAD THEY NOT BEEN FEELING something akin to romantic love for each other, those twelve people in the back dining room of that restaurant would have been most uncomfortable with their silence, nervous laughter and stealing glances at each other.

Finally someone asked, "What can twelve people do?"

Miz Whisnant's deep, mature laugh answered that.

"The story goes that Jesus made good use of twelve people," she said. Again they just looked at each other.

"If this is about Jesus, we may have a problem," Carol Tanic broke the silence again. "I know nothing about any of you, but because we have had similar experiences, I'm going to share with you very honestly. I hope I don't upset you or confuse you, but I just have to tell you that I am an atheist. I don't believe in a big man with a white beard who sits on a throne in the clouds. I read that 95 percent of all Americans believe in some kind of god, and that is fine with me. I have very deep and abiding faith in the most sacred things about life, in love and peace and joy and freedom, just to name my favorite four, and I believe those qualities of life are very sacred, precious, come from a very deep and meaningful place within us. I even pray, but I don't pray to a white-haired man in the clouds. I pray to my own sense of connection to everything, to subatomic structure, to natural law, to spiritual energy, that thing that rises up within me to meet itself rising up within others when we laugh or cry together or when we experience the best about life."

"Well, that doesn't sound very atheistic to me," Calvin Dart, the cab driver, offered. "In fact, it sounds just like the experience I had looking at the planter."

Others nodded their heads.

"Really?" Carol asked.

"Really," Dart answered. "The best in life, which I do identify with Jesus, but I can understand others do not, that is what I experienced as I looked at the planter. The best in life, yes that was it exactly, not fear or heartache or worry, but good feelings, the best feelings I have ever known."

"Maybe we could just get more people to view the planter," one of the college girls said.

"I think that is already happening," Miz Whisnant said.

Despite Russell Cambry and Billy Ray having more gravel hauled in, despite a number of cars parking on the road, despite getting some help from the local sheriff's department in directing traffic, after Russell had met with them and made a nice donation, the situation was getting out of hand.

W. Dixon and Russell had taken to sitting on either side of the planter and talking with people.

"I've got too much credit card debt," one man had confessed to the two men seated on either side of the planter.

"Of course, you have to stop spending money," W. Dixon said.

"I'm borrowing money at this point to pay the payments and eat and put gas in my car," the man said.

"How much could you afford to pay and not have to borrow more?" Russell asked.

"Maybe six or seven hundred a month," the man said.

"Which is it, six or seven?" Russell asked without sounding harsh.

"Six," the man confessed and hung his head in shame.

"And how much are you paying after you borrow more to make payments?" Russell asked.

"Close to two thousand," the man said without lifting his head.

"You're spending two thousand dollars a month on debt retirement and getting further in debt?" Russell asked.

"Yes," the man said.

"Why don't you declare bankruptcy?" Russell asked.

"I'm scared I won't be able to make it without borrowing more money, and they won't lend it to me if I declare bankruptcy," the man said.

Russell knew that wasn't true, but he didn't tell the man, because he also knew bankruptcy and more debt would not solve his problem.

"Why have you come here?" W. Dixon asked.

"I've heard this is a miracle place, that God is moving through this planter," the man said.

"I don't believe in God, but I don't believe in bankruptcy either," Russell said. "Now that you're here, have you learned anything? Have you felt anything different?"

The man looked up from hanging his head and stared at the planter.

"I'm not sure I've learned anything, but I feel like I can do anything. I feel like I have unlimited possibilities."

"Well, that's not true," Russell said.

"With God all things are possible," W. Dixon said.

"I'm a little more practical than that," Russell said. "You don't have unlimited possibilities, but you have a great many more choices that you can imagine when you're borrowing money to make payments on money you borrowed last month. That sort of feels like going down a drain hole, does it not?"

"Yes," the man said, but he was smiling as he looked at the planter. "It feels terrible to be so badly in debt and getting deeper every month, but it feels wonderful to stand here and look at this planter."

"Look at me for just a minute," Russell said.

"Okay," the man said, but he kept smiling. Russell smiled, too. "Here's my business card. Call me tomorrow and we'll meet and talk about how to get your debt rescheduled, get your payments down around six hundred a month, and get a commitment from you to not borrow any more money. How does that sound?"

"Thank you, sir," the man said, shook hands with W. Dixon and Russell and walked off the deck. Dozens of other people stood in the yard staring at the planter, smiling, some had lifted their eyes to the heavens to pray, others had tears running down their cheeks. Still others had stood for a while, then walked over to the snack trailer and ordered a cheeseburger.

W. Dixon could not be there all the time, nor could Russell. Each had lives outside their involvement with the planter. Other preachers had come and gone. A native healer had driven over from the mountains of Tennessee. He sat in a lawn chair in the yard and recommended herbal medicines to a few people who had come and gone. He stayed a couple of days, camped on the property, and left.

Nobody stayed long. Russell had hired a private security firm, and he and the Crenshaws had agreed nobody could stay long. Russell had brought in port-a-johns, but he was beginning to think they needed a longer-term solution. Every day more people came, and every day Russell wondered what to do next.

Often people did not step onto the deck and talk with W. Dixon or Russell or the Crenshaws, so there was time for W. Dixon and Russell to talk between themselves.

"How can you be so sure you're supposed to be involved with all this?" W. Dixon asked.

"How can you be so sure?" Russell asked.

"I asked you first," W. Dixon answered and beamed his Jimmy Carter grin.

Russell rubbed his hands together and dug his fingers into his eyes, ran his hands over his hair and blew a long sigh.

"It's like everything else in life, in my life anyway. I find myself in a car with friends, headed off on a trip or an evening out, and I have a moment of questioning everything. How did this happen? Who are these people? I look at my own wife sometimes, and wonder who she is, where did she come from, how did we find each other?"

"Could it be the will of God?" W. Dixon asked.

"That's your answer, and I understand it, but it doesn't work for me. I'm a Buddhist. I seek to do right for its own sake, to speak the right way, to work the right way for its own sake. I don't believe in God, and apparently the God you believe in can't be too upset with me because he hasn't made much of an effort to change me," Russell said.

"Maybe he's sent me to change you," W. Dixon said.

"That could happen, but don't bet the farm," Russell patted his knees and grinned back at W. Dixon's grin. "You asked me about my involvement here, and before you try to change me, let me just say this is an absolute mystery to me. These people, the Crenshaws are such nice people. That little girl really is very unusual, but I like all three of them very much. The little girl is a little unnerving, almost irritating."

"But you came over here before you knew anything about the Crenshaws," W. Dixon pointed out.

"People have been drawn here by this planter. I'm just one of them," Russell said.

"Do you think it is a contact point from an alien civilization?" W. Dixon asked grinning even more broadly.

"That thought has crossed my mind, and I'm sure it has occurred to other people, too," Russell admitted and laughed.

"What advantage would there be to an alien civilization to make our people feel better, more powerful, more capable of doing amazing things?" W. Dixon asked.

"Well, I'm not sure it is an alien civilization, but if it is, they might want us to be prepared for their arrival, so they are lifting our spirits, in a manner of speaking. If we are open to all kinds of possibilities, then we would be open to the possibility of welcoming them and working with them to create harmony between us and them," Russell speculated.

"Pretty far fetched, huh?" W. Dixon asked.

"A carpenter from Nazareth dying on a cross and rising on the third day to create a world religion is pretty far fetched in my book, so you're way ahead of the curve in my book already," Russell said.

"What about an Indian prince sitting under a bodhi tree and receiving enough wisdom to create a world religion?" W. Dixon asked.

"Good point," Russell agreed. "So is this planter another bodhi tree?"

"Or another dove descending from the clouds to point out the chosen one?" W. Dixon asked.

"Whatever it is, it is the most engaging experience so far in my life, and I've had a wonderful life," Russell said.

W. Dixon suggested, "Maybe the best is yet to come."

Kruba Krisida was a younger man than Lumkin had expected him to be. A temple zhao sounded like the kind of job title that might take a little age. Instead Krisida looked to be early 30's, trim, muscular, athletic, more like a movie star than a religious leader.

Through the jeep driver/translator their first conversation went something like this.

"You have come a long way. You need rest."

"Yes, but I have questions I am most eager to ask you."

"Eagerness can cause stress. You rest first, and we will talk when you have rested."

"I work for people who are also most eager to learn the answers to the questions I have come a long way to ask you."

"Maybe you should work for other people."

"Please let me ask you about a man named Dudley Dumpling, and then I will rest."

"It would be rude of me to answer your questions when you are not rested and feeling very anxious."

"It will only frustrate me further if you insist on making me wait when I have come such a long way."

"We will see about that. Please rest."

At which point, Krisida walked away and left his house boy to show Lumkin and his jeep driver where they might lie down for a while and have some tea.

Feeling an excitement like the joy one anticipates on the arrival of a lover, Carol Tanic continued to write in her book, "The Jesus Of My Imagination." On the night she returned home from dinner with Miz Whisnant and Dart, the Taxi Driver, and the other nine pilgrims, she wrote these words, "I believe in infinite possibilities, even though I believe in neither a theistic god, nor a hell of eternal damnation. I believe that all things are possible, as Jesus is credited with saying in the Gospels, but I believe that he could have meant to say, 'with love all things are possible,' instead of 'with God all things are possible.' What if the spirit that was embodied in the one called Jesus was a spirit of oneness instead of separation? What if that spirit, which has been perceived to have divided the world into the saved and the unsaved, instead united the world into a spiritual oneness that will certainly save all beyond death, and eventually even save the world from the curse of death itself, so that a heaven, or a nirvana, as the Buddhists call it, or a righteousness, as the ancient prophets called it, actually comes into being in this lifetime, among us, among our institutions and the scenes of our daily lives? That feels possible to me, especially since I believe in infinite possibilities."

She looked at that paragraph, and she liked it, and she said it was good. Her hand shook with joy as she saved the file on her computer, and crawled into her bed for a night's sleep.

Carol Tanic had not always been an atheist. In fact, she had been a United Methodist minister for ten years. She had not always been single. She was once married to Randy Perkins, the father of her 12-year-old son, Jake. As a minister, she had prayed to and believed in a very traditional God, a Biblical God. As a married woman, she had deferred to a fairly traditional husband, a liberal, a man who claimed to be a feminist, but a man with a singular view of reality that made him obsessed with being right. When Carol became addicted to prescription painkillers and lost custody of their son in the divorce, she had tried to explain to Randy about his obsession with being right. She told him four stories about times in their marriage when had been so obsessed that even their son had noticed.

Carol had sat on the edge of their marriage bed, and said, "Randy, I'm sorry about making fun of your not liking bluegrass in front of our friends. I'm sorry. I apologize."

At dinner the night before, Carol had talked about loving bluegrass music, and Randy had told everyone at the table that it drives him crazy. The high tempo banjoes and fiddles made him "want to jump out of his skin," as he put it, and the edge in his voice let Carol know it was coming from a deep place.

She snapped back, "Boy, that's news to me," and the edge in her voice had made Randy fall silent, leaving the rest of the dinner party to struggle along for a while as Randy stayed quiet.

On the way home, he said, "I don't want to fight about this, but I would appreciate it if you never spoke to me like that in front of our friends."

So she apologized. She felt weak and stupid for apologizing, like it might have been nice to talk about what went on. Carol knew Randy could only listen to a little bluegrass. At that point, they had been married for ten years. She always turned off the bluegrass if she had been listening to it and Randy came home. She never turned to the bluegrass radio station if Randy rode with her in the car. It was one of the sacrifices she made gladly because she loved Randy, and she believed Randy loved her.

But they both hated to fight, and one of Randy's ways of handling his hatred of fighting was to say something that was nonnegotiable by starting with, "I don't want to fight about this."

And Carol wouldn't fight. She would stuff her desire to talk things through, to get Randy to talk about their differences, and she would apologize, and the night she apologized to Randy over the bluegrass incident, Jake walked into their bedroom.

"Dad, don't you get it? You're always right. Mom's always wrong. She always apologizes," their son said.

It sent a surge of fear through Carol. She felt Randy had been outed by his beloved son. Her heart raced to hear what Randy would say when their dirty little secret had come out. Jake, at nine years old, had seen through the dirtiest glass in their marriage, the unspoken fact, the fact that nobody wanted to look at, the fact that Randy was always right.

Carol waited for a storm of denial, because as hip and easy going as Randy appeared to the rest of the world, he had a private fury that made Carol shudder like a trapped mouse. She sat on the edge of their bed and waited for an eruption.

"Have you finished your homework, big guy?" Randy asked.

Randy spewed no fury, no storm, no shouting and shaking of his finger. Carol did not look at her son. Years later she would weep with regret that she had not seized that opportunity to talk, to air the laundry, to give and take, and yes, maybe even fight about the fact that they both hated to fight. She would tell her friends years later, "a marriage is worth fighting for," but hers had not been that night or the dozens of other nights when Randy would make it quite clear he did not want to talk about anything that divided them, that pushed them apart.

He had veto power. He had a killer phrase that stopped them both from fighting. "I don't want to fight about this."

Carol had loved him as much as any man she had ever known. She had fallen so much in love that it never occurred to her not to marry him, not to give him a son, not to bet her life, her honor, her sacred fortune on a man she believed to be both beautiful and full of heart. She ignored so many danger signs, the fact that they both borrowed money whenever they pleased, always betting on the hope of a more lucrative future.

It was that lucrative future, and her conviction that the church would never share her vision of service to the poor, the outcast, especially gays, lesbians, Latinos, and anybody else on the fringe of society, that drove her to Charleston and attempt a career in insurance.

She believed the life of a minister was tough but rewarding. Days on end of hospital visits, time with the elderly, planning sermons, continuing education classes and readings, committee meetings, all that had been hard enough, but she found it rewarding. Selling insurance just turned out to be hard. She often muttered to herself, "If it were easy, everybody would do it."

And she felt betrayed, abandoned, and washed up by losing daily contact with her son, Jake. She and Randy had built a life in Rutherfordton, but the insurance job drew her four hours away in Charleston, S.C., the beautiful, historic city of narrow streets and heavy traffic, great food and ornate architecture, and a cosmopolitan population of people who shared her love of politics, social action, and multi-layered theologies.

All that was grand and glorious about Charleston could not substitute for the heartache she felt away from Randy and Jake, especially Jake, who was only six at the time of his mother's departure. The first night in Charleston, she sat in the parking lot of a Taco Bell and wept with Jake over her cell phone.

"I miss you, Mommie," the little boy cried.

"I miss you, too, baby," she answered. Her voice cracked and a high whine broke from her. She felt self-conscience and looked around the parking lot to see if she had drawn any attention. She had not. Two hundred and twenty miles from her husband and son, she was alone. "Such a dreamer," she chided herself for years after that night in the Taco Bell parking lot. Her dreaming heart believed Randy would sell the house and follow her to Charleston. Her dreaming heart believed she could build a successful insurance business, hire other agents, and even move into the local hubbub of politics and social action to create what she believed was the world she and Randy and millions of other people dreamed was possible, a world of peace and food and decent housing and schools and community health clinics.

An appointment with a Charleston dentist changed all that. While struggling to see prospects, write new business, find leads in the insurance business, she ground her teeth while sleeping and broke one. The repair job had turned into a root canal, and the dentist had prescribed oxycodin.

A man she had chatted with casually who often stayed in the same motel asked her what she had in her drug store bag. When she told him oxycodin or oxycotton, as it is known on the street, he grinned and plucked the bag from her hand.

"Let me show you a trick," he said and kept grinning as he motioned her into his room. "You can leave the door open. I'm harmless."

She thought to herself he might not be harmless, but she was pretty fast on her feet and there were always plenty of friendly folks around the motel parking lot, so no big risk. She did leave the door open.

The man shook two pills from the bottle and crushed them under a metal spoon on his bathroom counter. He raked the powder into a glass and dissolved it in a splash of Gatorade.

"Don't use soda. Carbonation can cut the power," he said and offered her the glass.

"Why did you crush them?" she asked downing the drink.

"It gets rid of the time released elements. You're in pain. You don't want to have to wait for relief," he said and pointed toward her room. "Better go lie down. You don't want to start feeling pain free with a cute man like me hanging around."

As she smiled and nodded, he opened his palm.

"Think you could spare a couple of those?" he asked, and she nodded again, but definitely felt like lying down after a long day of selling and a couple of hours in the dentist chair.

Chapter Six

LUMKIN SAT ACROSS FROM KRISIDA at a traditional Thai dinner.

"Sir, with all due respect, I am simply seeking information about a man who called himself Dudley Dumpling," Lumkin said with exasperation. The dinner was on its fourth course, and Krisida had spoken of nothing but the beauty of the temples, inquiries about Lumkin's travel, and a dozen other subjects that struck Lumkin as small talk and nothing more.

"Respect is a very important word," Krisida said and smiled and sipped from his teacup.

Lumkin looked at him and realized the man had no intention of answering any questions until he was ready.

"Tell me more about that," Lumkin said with resignation. He felt tired, cranky, irritated, and wanted nothing more or less than information leading to the arrest and trial of the software engineer who had cost his company six million dollars.

"Respect is woven into everything. A tree cannot live without leaves to gather the sunlight and use its power to convey life, but the leaves must have the stems by which the branches bring them water and combine the life energy in the water with the power of the sun. And the branches must have the limbs and the limbs must have the trunk and the trunk must have the roots, which need dirt and water. Air, water, light, power, there is no separation in that system, no jealousy, no conflict, only respect. The limbs never go to war with the roots."

Lumkin wanted to strangle the man or beat his face with his fists. What in the name of sweet, baby Jesus was the point of overstating the obvious? What in the Sam Hill good would come of his listening to a biology lesson on leaves and trees?

"Why do you push?" Krisida asked him.

"I'm not sure I understand the question," Lumkin answered.

"You have been here only hours. You took rest. We are having dinner together, and yet you seethe like a trapped rat to get what you came for and move on. I might learn something from you, but you give me no time to learn about you, to hear your stories, to find what truth might lie within you," Krisida chided with a soft voice and a gentle smile.

"I just came here for one simple piece of information," Lumkin said and opened his hands as if to say he overstated the obvious.

"No one ever goes anywhere seeking one simple piece of information. When I rise from my bed to piss in the morning, I am not simply seeking a place to piss. I am seeking my breath and the light by which to see. I keep a book of Keats poems by my bed and sometimes seek Keats as I piss. I seek memories of my dreams and dreams of making even more memories. You, in fact, are not seeking one simple piece of information," Krisida paused for a sip of tea and a bite of cake.

Lumkin leaned forward to speak, but Krisida held up his hand to stop him.

"You needed rest after a long journey, and I gave you a place to rest. You needed food, and I have fed you, and though you may never acknowledge it, you are seeking light to see by, light for the soul, connection between that which is highest within you and that which is highest in all of life, even in death and pain and suffering."

What a load of crap, Lumkin felt, but did not say.

"The modern way is always to push. You push yourselves out the door in the morning, push yourselves into cars, trains, planes, and push yourselves out of these transporters into offices and factories and stores and hospitals and parks and movie houses as if any of these might give you what you are pushing for, and you think it is your idea."

"Our idea?" Lumkin asked without realizing he was being taken in by this Buddhist zhao.

"Yes, you imagine this is what you want, this what you have imagined for yourself. But it is not. Our lives are not our lives. Our lives are the work of everything around us. We no more dream this stuff up than the leaf on the tree dreams the tree. We are the products of forces as old as the universe and as fresh as the morning dew. We come out of the trillions of incidents that made up the lives of our ancestors, and the intentions of engineers that make the traffic lights turn red and green. It is always happening to us so much more than we are making it happen, so the most powerful thing we can do is allow it to happen, to ride it like a drop of rain rides the sky until it strikes that leaf on that tree then falls to the ground and soaks the roots. We are raindrops, Mr. Lumkin, so much more than we are people who can fly to Thailand and find Dudley Dumpling," Krisida said.

"Do you know where he is?" Lumkin asked.

"You have not heard a word I have said," Krisida mused and threw back his head to laugh with joy. "Talking to you is like petting a dog. There will never be enough."

"Do you know where he is?" Lumkin asked.

"Ah, my dear, dear, Mr. Lumkin, you are asking the wrong question, and when you are asking the wrong question, I fear there will never be a right answer, regardless of how many times you ask it," he said with his infuriating smile. He stood from the table. "Come, let's got for a walk."

The oxycotton took her like a bird in flight. She took to it, like a nap on a warm afternoon. Her dreams of balancing a life of business and politics and social action in the beautiful, Southern city of Charleston melted into nothing but dreaming.

Instead of walking the streets of Charleston neighborhoods for politicians she admired and causes she loved, she simply dreamed of those walks and causes. Instead of making phones calls, stuffing envelopes, sending emails, and attending receptions for the local no-kill animal shelter, the organic food co-op, the gay and lesbian rights organization, and the mothers against the war, she scored her favorite powder, went to sleep, and dreamed of saving the world.

Randy would awaken her sometimes for her nightly phone calls, and she had a remarkable capacity to act as though nothing was wrong, everything was fine. A little grogginess in her voice would be explained away as napping after a long day.

And she loved talking to Jake.

"Hey, baby," she would coo into the phone.

"Hey, Mommie," her little boy would say, and they both fought tears.

She often hung up the phone and heard a voice instead her say, "You have lost your mind. You have lost whatever little mind you ever had."

And Carol would often asked herself, "Who is that voice in your head? My brother maybe?"

When Carol decided to leave the United Methodist Church and sell insurance in Charleston, 220 miles from her son and husband, her brother, Charles, the one the family called "Champ," had asked her, "Have you lost your mind?"

Or was it the voice of God?

Now there's a Jim Dandy question for an ex-minister, drug addict, on the way to becoming an atheist having a mystical experience with a planter.

Was it the voice of God?

No, not for Carol Tanic. It was not the voice of God. The God she had loved and worshipped as a United Methodist was a loving God. He would not growl at her across the cosmos, using his mean and angry voice and ask, "Have you lost your mind?" That was not the God she worshipped.

Her God would have been much nicer.

Her God would have said, "Carol, honey, we need to talk."

So whose voice was it?

Maybe it was the voice of reason. Reasonable, practical, decent, upstanding people had given their lives to balancing her zeal.

She believed in planetary transformation, a day to come when everybody would have enough to eat, a decent work, basic education and health care and no one would study war any more.

"You really believe that?" friends and family and coworkers would ask her.

"Yes," she answered over and over. "I really believe that."

And for four months the oxycotton had derailed that train. For four months the train had left the track of her daily life and rolled into her dream world. Mostly, she slept. She sold enough insurance to support her habit, bathed, dressed, and slept.

She called on a nurse at the Navy's hospital in Charleston. The woman was a prospect for one of her policies.

"Sixth door on your left. She told us you were coming," another nurse told her when she arrived on the appointed floor.

Carol had never been that good with numbers, so she failed to count to six. She stepped into the wrong room and recoiled at the sight of a young marine who had lost an arm and a leg from a roadside bomb in Iraq. "I'm sorry," she forced herself to say, before back peddling like a scalded dog. She felt bile rising in her throat, but swallowed quickly in hopes of controlling it. She looked around wildly, but remembered to breathe. She thought of Jake, and caught hold of his face in her mind, her little boy, her magical son, thank God, Jake, hey, Jake, Jake the sailor man. She had called him that when he was very small, a little bitty boy, Jake, Jake, the sailor man.

"Miss Tanic?" the nurse she was supposed to see spoke as she stepped into the hall.

"Yes," Carol nodded and took another deep breath. She concentrated on her son's face in her mind.

"Are you okay?" the nurse asked.

"I just got disoriented," Carol answered. "I'm fine now. Can we use this office?"

They met for the usual half hour it took Carol to explain the policy and answer questions. The woman liked what she heard, as so many of her prospects did, and signed the necessary paper work.

During the half hour, as Carol had been going through a routine she knew without thinking, her mind had switched between the young marine who was only a few feet away from them and her son, Jake. That half hour had convinced her to kill the monster that was pouring oxycotton down her throat like the devil's milkshake.

"I'm supposed to be working to end this war," she kept hearing in her head as she saw the marine, saw her son, saw the marine, saw her son.

She packed up the nurse's paper work, took a small check, a deposit on the policy, thanked her and rode the elevator to the main lobby.

"I need to talk to a chaplain," the ex-minister told the receptionist.

The chaplain greeted her warmly after what felt like a long wait. His office was small, his bookshelves crammed.

"Twelve steps," Carol said after quick pleasantries.

The young chaplain frowned as though he did not understand.

"I'm a drug addict, parson. When and where is the next 12-step meeting?" she asked.

She had attended many meetings as a minister. Other addicts had come to her in similar straights, and she had gone with them to listen to stories, to learn the 12 steps, to "work the program," as they call it.

The fist step is to admit that your life is out of control.

In the basement of a Charleston church house, within two hours of meeting with the chaplain, Carol Tanic said those words, "My life is out of control."

Carol's memory of it is surreal, like pancake batter or mixing paint. She admits her life is out of control, and it begins to be in control, but control by whom? She admits the need for a higher power, but becomes an atheist, so must find that higher power within her self. And if it is within her self, it is higher than what? And what are the differences among: her life, the one who loses control of her life, the higher power, and the cocktails of oxycotton that send her off to sleep with dreams of being the person she dreams of being when her life is not out of control? Who is she, what is the drug, and who or what is the higher power?

The pancake batter keeps stirring in the bowl. The paint keeps mixing in the can.

In the weeks that followed she attended a meeting a day, which is standard for the 12-step recovery programs whether you are recovering from addiction to alcohol, drugs, gambling, sex, sugar, spice, or everything nice.

In the second step, she affirmed her belief that a higher power could restore her to sanity, but she wondered what sanity would look like. She stopped using, which meant often not answering the door to her motel room, which often meant listening to knock after knock, which sometimes meant walking up to the door and saying, "If you don't stop knocking, I will call the police."

And sometimes she had to say that more than once. She did not believe the people who sold her the drugs were evil. She did not believe she was evil for buying the drugs, but she came to believe both were boring, and never had anything in her life felt as horrible and unnerving and alienating as boredom. Having spent part of her life as a minister and part of her life as a newspaper reporter, she always knew she could write. Writing had been her salvation, although she had once heard that Thomas Merton considered himself an addict to writing, that he would force himself to stop writing, to go for long walks, to pray, to look at the world around him, to talk with other monks in the monastery where he lived, to work in the garden, to wash the dishes, to do anything to keep himself from writing. Carol felt surprised by that, because she likes to read his writing, but having done a lot of writing in her life, she remembered thinking, "Writing and reading are two entirely different things."

Suddenly in working the 12 steps, she was bored. So many of the stories sounded the same. "I sold my wedding ring to buy crack." "I sold my kid's GI

Joe collection to buy booze." "I sold my ass to buy heroine." "I sold my heroine to buy more ass."

Her dream world had been so much better than her recovery world. She had liked politics and social action, going to meetings and walking the street for great causes; but she had liked dreaming about it even more. "Just let me go back to sleep," she had begged her recovering self. Her dreaming self wanted to go back to sleep, not back to the streets and the meetings and the conversations about the streets and the meetings and the conversations about having more conversations.

It was just so boring to work her insurance business, which she continued to do, go to 12-step meetings, which she continued to do, and go back to her flea bag motel and beg herself not to watch television, not to read trash novels, not to write self-pitying diatribes in her notebooks. It was boring, boring, boring.

Home on the weekends, she put up a good front. Randy was a social worker, who spent many hours filling out paper work for the Medicaid system. He would say later that he saw the changes in Carol, both during her period of using drugs and her recovery, but his overwhelming workload, caring for Jake, and that fact that his invalid father, Arthur Connelly, lived with the family, all combined to take up so much of his attention that he was pressed hard to notice Carol slipping away from him.

And Carol hated slipping away. She had gone to Charleston to establish herself in business, not to lose her marriage to Randy. Nobody sets out to become either a drug addict or a recovering addict on a path that leads to divorce. Sometimes things just happen. Carol could recall seeing the bumper sticker that reads, "Shit happens," and thinking, "That would be true."

She also liked the bumper sticker that reads, "Grace happens," but she hadn't seen so many of those.

The third step of recovery requires the surrender of will to God, as the recovering addict understands God.

Here began Carol's path to atheism. She couldn't understand God. She had loved God, worshipped God, prayed to God, and led other people in the traditional United Methodist worship of God, but sitting in that church basement, amid cinder block walls and Styrofoam cups of coffee, she purely and simply lost all understanding of God.

"I don't understand you, God," she had said in her head. "I don't understand the great waves of human cruelty you have sat by and watched happen. How could you allow the Reformation for starters or even further back, how could you insist that the Jews kill all those people in the Bible? Why did you punish King

Saul for not killing every woman and child and slave among the enemy? You were a war criminal in those old stories. And while I am bitching and moaning, let me just throw in here, how could you let me become a drug addict? Me, God, how could you let someone who is a liberal Democrat become a drug addict, even the same drug Rush Limbaugh got addicted to? Is that like some kind of cosmic joke? I'm the one who believes every social problem can be solved if we just apply enough will and love and planning? You don't need me addicted to drugs, God. You need me out in the street organizing and raising money and passing out brochures and making speeches and rallying the faithful. Come on, God, what were you thinking when you let the cavalry kill all those Indians and what were you thinking when you let little old Carol Tanic fall apart and become a drug addict? Come on, God, I need some answers. I need a miraculous manifestation of the spiritual energy it will take to overcome evil in the world and make me stop mixing oxycotton with Gatorade for Pete's sake."

The silence was so cold and pining over her head and under her feet and down in the pit of her stomach that she finally realized there must not be a God there, not the God of the old Hebrew stories, not the God of the cavalry that killed the Indians, not the God of the Holocaust, not the God who let the Yankees win the World Series so many times, no God, just not a God, not one single God who straddled the universe while stringing all those stars and raising up all those mountains. Nope, that God just isn't there.

So how was she supposed to work the third step of the 12-step program? She decided to create a picnic basket of gods. She put hope and love and joy and freedom and common sense in her picnic basket. She wrapped up common sense in waxed paper and snuggled it into her basket. She thought about humor and stuffed in a jar of that. She asked herself, "How can anybody be a recovering addict without a sense of humor?" She felt that love would cover caring, affection, attention to detail, and perhaps that ache in her heart every time she realized how much she missed Jake and wanted to hold him in her arms.

That would do it, by golly. She would pack a picnic basket with enough gods to put the old God to shame, and she would worship all that, turn her life over to all that, and instead of living a willful, egocentric, drug addicted life, she would become a third-step recovering addict with a picnic basket under arm.

She thought of Dorothy Gale of Kansas and wondered if there would be room in her basket for Toto.

Step four required a thorough and searching moral inventory.

Carol Tanic could imagine nothing more challenging, more stressful, or more discouraging than a thorough and searching moral inventory.

Krisida and Lumkin walked the mountain paths around the temple at Wat San Phra Chao Dang. Birds of every color perched and flew above their heads. Monkeys called to each other in a language that Krisida suspected spoke of the foolish humans on the path below, and lizards hung to rocks in the sun.

"I think that Dudley Dumpling may be the man you seek," Krisida finally told Lumkin as they rounded yet another bend in the forest path, a bend that Lumkin feared might lead to another bend.

"How is that possible? You know nothing of why I seek him," Lumkin said and heard something more settled, less irritated in his voice. Had the monk finally worn him down to the point that he could tolerate all the waiting that Krisida had insisted was important.

"I know you work for Consolidated Insurance Company," Krisida said.

"Yes, but how is that related to Dudley Dumpling or whatever this man's name really is?" Lumkin asked.

"Hasn't Consolidated Insurance distributed some refund checks to certain individuals in the southeastern mountains of your country?" Krisida asked.

Lumkin stopped walking. He blew a long breath and fished a handkerchief from his hip pocket. He mopped the back of his neck and his forehead.

"How could you possibly know that?" Lumkin asked.

"It's on the Internet. The Associated Press carried the story a few weeks ago. You didn't see it?" Krisida asked and smiled as if that truly surprised him.

"The Associated Press has carried a story about our company issuing refund checks?" Lumkin rephrased the question so as to only repeat the information Krisida had conveyed to him and to add no details of his own.

"Yes," the monk concurred without conveying any more information.

"What did the story say?" Lumkin asked suddenly feeling very foolish for not having knowledge of the story.

"It said 16 people had received the refund checks and by some rather bizarre twist of fate, they had also traveled to the home of a couple outside some small town and spent time staring at a terra cotta planter on the deck of the couple's home," Krisida said. "I thought that might have something to do with Dudley Dumpling and why you had come, but you didn't know about the story?"

Lumkin stood in the forest path for a moment as though he had suddenly been confronted with words spoken in a foreign tongue.

"A terra cotta planter?" Lumkin asked.

"Yes, I believe it's gray with ivy growing out of it," Krisida said.

"Do you perhaps have a copy of this Associated Press story?" Lumkin asked.

"Oh, better than that," Krisida answered. "I can show you a web site that has gone up that shows the planter to the whole world." Krisida rang out a high giggle, and added, "Or at least those of us who have access to the Internet."

Miz Whisnant sat in front of her home computer answering dozens of emails from what was becoming an unmanageable Internet social network. It was comprised of people who had seen the planter or seen the web site that she and Russell Cambry had launched to celebrate the planter and people who had received refund checks from Consolidated Life.

So far, they had found 783. Miz Whisnant was intrigued to note they all lived in the mountains of North and South Carolina and Virginia. She found that worthy of note.

She bowed her head and prayed to a carpenter who had been killed two thousand years earlier for allegedly offending the local authorities by claiming to be the Jewish Messiah. Some controversy remains as to whether he was the Jewish Messiah or whether he claimed to be.

"Lord Jesus," she began to pray, "I just want to humble myself before you and admit that there is a whole lot more going on here than I can understand or even perceive. I have lived my whole life, Jesus, trying with all my might to be used by you, to get myself out of the way and let you have full reign in my humble heart and pitiful little old life. But Lord God Jesus, I have to admit you have done come up in here and blown this old lady's mind. Come now by the power of the Holy Spirit and help me have just the tiniest notion of what all I am supposed to do. It is in your precious and holy and righteous and powerful and almighty name that I pray. Amen and amen."

Her telephone rang. It was Jenifer Davis calling from her office at The Daily Courier.

Lisa Crenshaw walked her twelve-year-old, adorable self onto the deck to find Russell Cambry seated by the planter. The seat normally held by W. Dixon was vacant, so Lisa hopped into that chair.

"If you could feed all the children in the world, Mr. Cambry, all the children who don't have enough to eat, would you do it?" Lisa asked.

"Of course, I would," Russell answered and smiled at the little girl who had challenged so much of his worldview.

"So, why don't you?" she asked.

"I don't know how," he answered and opened his hands as if to say the problem remains quite a challenge.

"Aren't you rich?" she asked.

"Yes, Lisa, I am very, very rich. I'm worth millions of dollars, but even if I gave away all my money, there would still be hungry children in the world," he said.

"Why don't you ask your rich friends to help you?" she asked.

"Well, now you're getting somewhere, young lady," Russell answered. He had a deep baritone that sounded like a radio announcer or a minister, even though he was a Buddhist and therefore did not believe in God. "That's what Bill and Melinda Gates and Warren Buffet are doing. Their work is not only spending lots of money on problems like hunger, but it's challenging other rich people to do the same."

"So, why isn't it working?" Lisa asked.

"Well, we don't know that it isn't working," Russell answered. "You're talking about something that is hard to measure. There are still some terrible wars going on in Africa and south Asia where a lot of the hunger is. But there are many groups like Doctors

Without Borders and others who are doing some wonderful work where people are hurting the most. It just takes time to measure the good people do. When somebody does something bad, the evidence is right there, whether it is a murder or a divorce or a fire or a bomb blowing something up. But when somebody does something good, it's just harder to measure."

"Do you think you have done all the good you could do?" Lisa asked.

"No, Lisa, I'm sorry to say I have not. I wish I had. I wish every time a good opportunity came along, I jumped on it with both feet, but I did not and do not," Russell admitted.

"Well, you did good when you helped my mommie and daddy deal with this planter thing," Lisa said.

He sat smiling and laughing softly at the charming young woman whose company came so easy to him. He was still pretty sure she had to occasionally break wind like the rest of the human race.

"And you will do a lot more good things before you die," Lisa said.

He narrowed his eyes and stopped smiling.

"What makes you say that? I could die in the next few days and do nothing else good," he offered.

"Can I tell you a secret, Mr. Cambry?" she asked.

"Do I have to promise to keep it a secret, Lisa?" he asked.

"That's a hard promise to keep, Mr. Cambry," she said.

"Well, I guess if you know that and are still willing to risk that I might tell someone, sure, tell me a secret," he said.

"I know the future."

"You've known the whole time why I came," Lumkin said.

"Not exactly," Krisida disagreed and shook his head. "But I knew Dudley Dumpling had once worked for an insurance company in the United States. He had told me that. He was a man of great mystery, kept to himself, spoke little, but I knew he was an unusual person just from the way he walked and the look in his eye."

"So where is he?" Lumkin asked.

"Africa," Krisida said.

"Where in Africa?" Lumkin asked.

"Or China or Russia or India or Bolivia," Krisida said and smiled. "He could be anywhere people are hurting. He likes to help people who are hurting."

"You have no idea where he is," Lumkin said.

"None," Krisida agreed.

"And do you know who he lived with when he was here, any clue that might help me find him?" Lumkin asked.

"I know nothing," Krisida said.

"You know nothing or you are unwilling to say?" Lumkin asked.

Krisida stood from his desk, where he had shown Lumkin the web site for the planter, and moved to his stove to heat water for tea. Lumkin watched the muscular young man move with a grace and energy he envied. Outside in the courtyard children played and laughed, chickens chased each other, and sunlight played on the afternoon scene.

"Which is it?" Lumkin asked. "You don't know or you won't say?"

"You are so impatient, worse than most Americans," Krisida said without a hint of irritation or judgment, just stating what he observed.

"There is a great deal of money involved here," Lumkin said.

"I can't measure money. It is one thing one day and another thing another day. Exchange rates change. The price of oil changes. We grow most of our own food, and the water comes to us for free. We don't use as much money as you do, although I did use money for my computer, and I do pay money for the electricity to run it and my refrigerator. I don't understand how money works. You spent a great deal of money to come here?"

"Yes," Lumkin answered and wondered where the conversation was going. "Several thousand dollars."

"More money than I spend in a year you spent in a week or ten days to come here," Krisida said.

"I'm looking for a man who stole six million dollars from my company," Lumkin said.

"Dudley Dumpling stole six million dollars from your company and put it in a bank account so he could come to Thailand and live with mountain villagers?" Krisida asked.

Lumkin shook his head.

"Not exactly," Lumkin admitted.

"Then what?" Krisida asked.

"He caused those refund checks to be mailed," Lumkin said.

"Those 16 people in North Carolina who ended up staring at that planter got six million dollars?" Krisida asked.

"No, not those 16 people," Lumkin said.

"Who then?" Krisida asked and poured the water into the teapot.

"Many more than those 16 people," Lumkin said.

"How many more?"

"26,000."

Krisida laughed and placed the teapot on a tray with cups and cakes.

"So your company now has no money?" Krisida asked.

"No, we still have money," Lumkin said.

"How much?" Krisida asked.

"Billions of dollars to insure our customers," Lumkin said.

"You have billions of dollars to insure your customers. How many customers do you have?"

"Millions," Lumkin said and popped one of the small cakes into his mouth. It was soft and sweet.

"Millions of customers and billions of dollars and you travel to the other side of the world looking for a man who gave away six million dollars? Why do you care?" Krisida asked.

"He's a thief," Lumkin said.

"No, I don't think so. A thief doesn't steal money for other people. He steals money for himself. I believe Dudley must be some other kind of man," Krisida speculated, but shrugged as if it didn't matter.

"What if he had stolen it from you?" Lumkin asked.

"If I had thousands of chickens and a man stole six of them to give to other people, I might want to have tea with him, so he could explain to me why he had done it," Krisida said and nodded.

"Well, I guess we are a little like that," Lumkin said and laughed. "We'd at least like to have tea with him and ask him why he did it."

Krisida laughed along with Lumkin. They felt like they understood each other a little better as they laughed together.

"I believe if I were you, and certainly I am not you," Krisida began still laughing as he stood by the stove waiting for the water to boil. "I believe I would give up the search for Dudley Dumpling and go, instead, to North Carolina and talk with the people who received the checks and gather around the planter. Maybe they hold the answer you are looking for."

Lumkin thought about that. He would discuss it with his boss.

"Well," Russell Cambry murmured to the little girl who sat across the planter from him, "if you can tell the future, why don't you tell me who's going to win the world series next year, and we'll bet enough money to cure world hunger."

She laughed and laughed.

"Oh, Mr. Cambry, that isn't the kind of future I can tell," she said gasping for breath. "But that was a very funny question you asked me."

"What kind of future can you tell?" Russell asked.

"I don't know how to explain it. I just look at you and I see things about you and Mr. W. Dixon and my parents and that woman Carol Tanic. You are all going to have a wonderful time together for a long time to come," she said so confidently that Russell felt swept up in her spirit, her joy, her beautiful, freckled face.

"That's perfectly delightful, dear," Cambry said. "Are we going to figure out how to solve the problems of the world?"

"Haven't we always known how to do that?" she asked.

"I don't know what you mean," he admitted.

"Haven't we always known that love would solve all the problems in the world?" she asked.

"I think it's a little more complicated than that," he insisted.

"And isn't it thinking things are complicated that makes them complicated? Wouldn't things be much simpler if we simply looked for simple answers instead of complicated answers?" she asked.

He sighed. He had many fascinating experiences in his long and successful life, but this girl, this planter, this stretched him like nothing else.

Jenifer told Miz Whisnant she had been contacted by a television producer named Stinson Q. Workman.

"Am I supposed to be impressed by that name?" Miz Whisnant asked in her least confrontational voice.

"He produces Dream Song for the Bull Network," Jenifer explained.

"I'm afraid I don't watch much television, but I have heard of Dream Song. It's that show where young people compete to be pop singers?" Miz Whisnant asked.

"Yes," Jenifer agreed and wondered how anybody could live in contemporary America and not know Dream Song. "Well, he's heard about the planter and he wants to produce a reality TV show around the people who have been affected by the planter."

"Oh, dear," the retired teacher moaned her reluctance. "That sounds a tad bit tacky somehow."

"He has an almost unlimited amount of money to spend on the project," Jenifer added.

The teacher paused. She hesitated to ever say anything negative about anybody or any situation. Good manners had been highly stressed to her as a young child, and she had only rarely departed from the practice.

"I don't believe that would mitigate my reluctance," she finally articulated as carefully as she could.

"He's sending someone from his office to visit the planter, and I hope I didn't make a terrible mistake. I gave him your name," Jenifer apologized.

"You have committed me to nothing, sweetheart. I'm sure I can handle myself just fine," Miz Whisnant said in her soft, rich voice.

Chapter Seven

THE SOMEONE FROM STINSON Q. Workman's office turned out to be Andrea Quigley, a red-haired granddaughter of Ireland, tiny, wide eyed and intense as the pilot light in a gas heater. She paused in Miz Whisnant's front yard like a China doll, before walking up to the door and knocking soundly.

Miz Whisnant, several inches taller and pounds heavier, greeted the young woman with her usual grace and manners.

"Do you care for pound cake, Miss Quigley?" Miz Whisnant asked.

"I really need to get down to business," Andrea Quigley said without using any form of direct address, a disconcerting habit practiced by residents of more urbane environments.

"Usually folks say, 'No thank you,'" the aged teacher offered almost without thinking.

"I beg your pardon," the emissary from television land said.

"In this part of the country, when someone offers someone pound cake and they don't care for any, they usually say, 'No thank you,'" the teacher taught.

Andrea Quigley dropped her eyes down onto a notebook she had balanced on one knee. Her slender, pale legs, extended before her from beneath a tight skirt that she somehow managed to use while both sitting and walking, although Miz Whisnant was not sure how.

"My employer is prepared to spend millions in your community to produce a reality television show about this planter and the ways in which it has affected so many people who live here. We understand you have taken a leadership role among the people who have spent time with the planter, and we are prepared to pay you handsomely for a consulting role on the show," Andrea flipped a pen in her hand as she spoke and when she finished she smiled tightly.

Miz Whisnant stood from her living room easy chair and walked to her picture window, which looked out onto the front yard Andrea had just crossed to enter her modest Polkville home. She looked out at the driveway where Andrea had parked the rental car she had driven in from the airport, a late model BMW roadster, not the least expensive car the rental company had available.

"When I was four years old, my mother worked for a white woman in Rutherfordton. She cleaned and cooked for the woman who paid her the going rate, maybe three or four dollars a day. Mother rode to Rutherfordton with three other domestics who took turns driving their husband's cars or farm trucks to save on gas and expenses. Mother often left me with a neighbor lady, too old to clean and cook for white folks, but on a particular winter morning I was sick with a fever and stomach bug, so Mother took me to work with her, carried me up to the back of that white lady's house and told her I was sick, too sick to leave with the neighbor lady. I think my mother may have thought I was so sick, I might not make it. She may have overreacted.

"The white lady was standing on her back porch and she barely looked at me. Like I said, I was four years old, but I can remember it like it was yesterday. She said, 'Put her there,' and pointed to an old sofa on the back porch where her dog slept. I know her dog slept there, because she had to move the dog out of the way to put me on the sofa. The dog snarled a little, but he moved. Mother had brought a big quilt from home, and had me all wrapped in it. I stayed pretty warm most of the day, but I wondered why I couldn't go inside where it was heated. Mother tended to me and kept a little bucket by that dog sofa in case I needed it. After lunch, the white lady must have felt bad knowing how sick I was, so she brought a little plate of cookies out to me on the back porch. Mother was right behind her, looking over her shoulder. The lady held out the plate to me, but my stomach hurt so bad I just shook my head to turn her down. Mother reached around that woman and slapped me hard on my little four-year-old arm and snapped at me, 'Abigail, you say 'No thank you,' and I could tell she was mad enough to keep on slapping my arm until I did. Oh, Andrea, I pushed my lips together as hard as I could and I took a deep breath to keep from crying, and said, 'No thank you.' After they had gone back inside I buried my little head in that quilt, and I cried like I was on fire. I hated disappointing my mother, and as I grew older and watched how relationships worked between black folk and white folk, I knew that basic good manners might mean as much as anything in showing people respect and being the kind of person my mother wanted me to be."

Andrea started to speak, but Miz Whisnant held up her hand to stop her. She walked back across the room and sat in her easy chair. She took her time walking and sitting and propped her arms on the cushioned arms of the chair. She let her fingers dangle in front of the arms of the chair and tipped her head to one side as she blinked and pursed her lips thoughtfully.

"Andrea, would you like a piece of my homemade pound cake?" she asked.

Andrea blinked and stared at the older woman and flipped her pen a few more times.

"No thank you," she said.

Miz Whisnant smiled.

"You learn fast, young lady. That's probably why Mr. Workman pays you the big bucks. Now, tell me how I can help produce your television show and why, besides getting paid, I would want to help you," she said.

The emissary from television was again taken aback. Ms. Whisnant impressed her with her strength and presence, but she was totally amazed by anyone who would question the taking of money as a sufficient motivation for action. In her world, most folks would do anything if there were enough money involved.

"The concept for our show is pretty standard reality television. We will establish a group of contestants who will face a number of tests competing for a prize of a million dollars," Andrea Quigly said.

"And what could that possibly have to do with me?" Miz Whisnant asked.

"We hope you would help us find some of our contestants and possibly be one yourself," Andrea spoke with flat tones and watched Miz Whisnant as she might watch an unusual insect that had crawled into her California home.

"You want me to eat bugs or race around the world?" Miz Whisnant asked.

Andrea smiled a quick turn of her lips and returned to her expressionless face.

"Our show is called 'The Million Dollar Dream.' Contestants will outline for our audience the extent of their dream for what they will do with the million dollars. They will then be placed in real life situations to test what it would be like to live that dream, and will be interviewed by our judges about how that dream compared to the reality. Pretty simple, huh? Each week two contestants will be asked to leave. In the final weeks the whole country will be asked to vote on who leaves and who stays," Andrea said.

Miz Whisnant eased back into her chair. She had been sitting very erect and had used her posture to challenge the young woman from California with the flat voice and matter-of-fact manner. Now, her resistance relaxed, and her body fell into thought, a rich thought.

"I know what I would do with a million dollars," she said after a moment of thought.

"Yes?" Andrea asked and turned her lips up into a smile again.

"I'd help poor children go to college," she said and let the words roll off her lips like the announcement of a new grandchild or news that the doctor says she doesn't have cancer.

Andrea's smile didn't change. "A lot of people would do that, in fact, have already done that, with large sums of money. I'm afraid we're looking for something a little different."

Miz Whisnant nodded and pressed her lips together to show a little frustration. "That's one of the problems with television. Always looking for something different, while real people in real life situations, are pretty much looking for what they've always looked for."

It was Andrea's turn to soften her body language a little. She rolled her shoulders and turned her head from side to side.

"You're probably right about that. What do you think real people in real life situations are looking for?"

"Something to eat, a decent place to live, a sense of connection to the world around them, maybe a little appreciation, a doctor when they're sick, and probably, with all due respect to the way you make your living, they're probably looking for something good to watch on television," she said, grinned widely and offered up soft laughter. "Of course, they say 'something good to watch,' but goodness often has nothing to do with it. What they are looking for is entertainment, distraction from the painful dullness of their own lives."

"Harsh," Andrea uttered.

"Maybe so, Miss Andrea, maybe so. Harsh perhaps. True, for sure," Miz Whisnant said and opened one hand of invitation. "How about that pound cake?"

"No, thank you," Andrea said and smiled even more widely.

"Good girl," Miz Whisnant affirmed. "I believe I'll have a piece."

The fifth step of 12-step recovery programs is to admit to God and ourselves the true nature of the harm we have done.

Carol Tanic had to admit she had lost her dream. Sleeping in flea bag motels, using thin towels after showering, listening to drunks argue in the parking lot and lovers grunt in the rooms next door, looking at stacks of insurance forms on the dresser across from her bed, she had to admit she had lost the vision, the desire, the sense that the world could be changed by an insurance lady who had left her young son and husband back in Rutherfordton, especially if that insurance lady spent every spare minute killing her pain with oxycotton.

She had not yet become an atheist, so she prayed. Prayer for her had become like trying to slide a wet noodle through a keyhole. She lay with her face in her pillow. She keened from the gut, hoped the pillow would muffle what sounded in her head like the desperate cries of a baby, wordless howls that tell the world something is badly wrong, no hope in sight, send the Marines, call the fire department, all is lost and not only can I not find it, but I cannot remember what it looked like.

Carol had spent a lot of her life thinking about God, the God of seminary classes, classic writing on the subject, shapeless, formless, ancient, open, arch of the rainbow, wet in the rain, darkness in the woods, shine in the sun, glitter, pitter patter, holy, holy, holy, Lord God Almighty.

But in the flea-bag, thin-towel, stacks-of-insurance-forms, motel-room desperation of a recovering addict, God became something she could not think about, but only hope to feel, pretty sure she would never feel again, still willing to throw one more pillow-muffled scream into the sheets.

She felt the sweat on her arms and down her back, hated the sense of sweat sticking her thin cotton gown to her sweaty, nasty back. Sweat on her legs, sticking to the sheets. God, come in, God. May Day! Both engines are on fire. Shit has hit the fan. Can't see, can't breathe. Wait! Can breathe. She sucked in a long breath and remembered stress management training. Breathe, you lousy piece of drug-sucking snail crap. Breathe, breathe, breathe, Carol, baby, sugar, breathe, come on, come on. God, living God, great God Almighty, Uncle Joe, moving kinda slow, Mark Twain, Granddaddy, who are you, where are you, can you hear me? I have lost my ever-loving mind. I am completely and totally and let me repeat myself, out of it.

God, I have hurt everybody I ever cared about. That is the exact nature of my wrongs. In Jesus' name I pray. Amen.

She drove home the next day to hear her husband say he wanted a divorce.

She looked at him like he had lost his mind, but he put it pretty plain and simple. "Don't try to deny it. You're a drug addict. You told me you were a recovering alcoholic when we married. You'll just keep doing it. I don't want to grow old with a drug addict tied around my neck. I don't want it for my son. Don't try to get custody. I'll hang your drug-addicted ass out to dry. Now, get the hell out of my house."

She spent the night on a friend's couch and wondered what the sixth step of recovery might be like. It would take her wrestling through quicksands of denial, but she would figure it out. Reading Bishop John Shelby Spong, she figured out that God was the wrong word for what she needed. The sixth step of the 12-step regime is to be willing to have God remove every defect of character, but she had been raised with a God who showed up in Bible stories and sat on a throne in the sky. In her sixth decade, a nice place, she noted, for the sixth step to take place, she had read and studied and looked at enough pictures made by telescopes to figure out that the sky is full of stars, not an old man with a white beard who showed up in Bible stories. She used a brain born in the twentieth century and now mucking about in the twenty-first century to figure away any chariots of fire, angels carrying swords of fire, fire from heaven. She had warmed herself by enough fires to think herself into believing fire was much more likely to come from dry wood dragged out of the forest than from the sky. She thought and figured and looked and studied and decided Joshua did not fight the battle of Jericho and the walls did not come tumbling down.

But giving up on the God of the Bible stories did not cause her to give up on the belief that there was something beyond her mind, her reason, her looking and thinking and figuring that might be able to heal her of her addiction to Oxycotton. She came to believe a power greater than herself could remove her defects of character.

As she continued to drive her car, visit her son, care for her aging mother, sell insurance, listen to National Public Radio, and read as much as she could find about alternative spirituality, she remembered her days as a Methodist preacher, her years as a Bible believing Methodist, her Sunday School teachers and preachers she had known and loved, and although she had given up the old man on the throne in the sky, she began to put her fingers around a power greater than herself, something beyond her ego, her pride, her pain at getting divorced (she cried and slammed her fist into the mattress of her divorced-person's apartment, as her landlord explained so many of them were,) as all of that was happening, a new spirit life was being born in her awareness. It felt not so much like a thought, but more as a presence. She had always believed Jesus walked with her, and as she gave up so much of her Bible story, Sunday School religion, she found a presence, shaped and silent and solid that bore a remarkable resemblance to a long-haired, bearded Jewish carpenter.

"This makes no sense," she would remind herself. But she often turned in the direction of the presence, a direction she began to feel stood by her in every direction, and she began again to pray. Her prayers sounded like this, "This makes no sense, but I am willing for you remove all my defects of character."

And that, of course, is the seventh step, to ask God, Jesus, Moses, Allah, Quan Yin, Buddha, Krishna whatever name we use to tap that which we believe to be connected to all and everything, she asked that her defects of character to be removed.

Russell Cambry drove to Charlotte, the largest city near Rutherfordton and sat down with a staffer at the Chamber of Commerce.

"I know this is a terrible inconvenience, but I'm not really sure why I am here," Cambry admitted.

The middle-aged woman, who sat across from him, smiled politely, and asked, "How about a hint?"

"Are you familiar with the planter that is getting a little media attention in the mountains outside of Rutherfordton?" he asked.

The woman looked up, pursed her lips slightly, and looked back at Cambry.

"Not ringing any bells. Tell me more," she said.

"Several weeks ago people started showing up at the home of this young couple, Mary and Billy Ray Crenshaw, and staring at this planter Mrs. Crenshaw had placed on her deck. Apparently the planter has the power to speak to people at a deeply emotional level. If I were entirely honest with you, I'd have to admit that the planter has that affect on me. When

I look it, I feel a supreme sense of self confidence, as though I could do almost anything," he said.

The Chamber staff woman looked nervously around the room. They were sitting in the large lobby of the Chamber offices in downtown Charlotte, so there were plenty of people around, but she looked like she might need to call for help.

"I'm sorry. I know this sounds insane, but let me tell you what I'm looking for and maybe I can be on my way," Russell said blushing deeply. He couldn't remember feeling this awkward since asking for his first date in high school.

Her eyes met his again and she said, "I'm listening."

"I need to get the word out to people that there is something very dramatic and very beautiful happening around this planter. I need to communicate with lots and lots of people. There is a television producer who is looking at doing a reality TV show around the planter, but that will take at least a year, and I think this is a resource that people could use in very creative ways, right now. We have a web site and a web camera that shows people what the planter looks like 24 hours a day, seven days a week, but I really want to drive some eyes to the web site, and maybe even bring more visitors to the actual physical site."

The woman tipped her head to one side and shrugged.

"Sounds like you need an advertising agency. Several are members of the Chamber. I can give you a list, but I can't recommend one specifically, since we treat all Chamber members the same," she sounded more relaxed than she had looked a moment before.

"I've never used an advertising agency before. I made my money in manufacturing, and we always marketed in house. Does this really sound to you like a marketing question?" Cambry asked, and wondered to himself just what he was looking for, and as he had wondered since he first laid eyes on the planter, he wondered again just what was going on. How had this happened? What does it all mean?

"Well, you said you want more people to know about the planter and you want more people looking at your web site and more people visiting the physical site. It sounds like marketing to me," she offered.

He sat for a moment.

"Everything in this crazy country is marketed to pieces. This has to be about something else," he said and stood. "I apologize. I'm afraid I've wasted your time."

"No need to apologize," she shook his hand, but couldn't help looking at him as though he might have come from another planet.

Russell Cambry walked away from the Chamber office and up North Tryon Street in the main business section of the city among giant steel and glass structures not unlike those of other cities. He questioned himself. Why had he driven to Charlotte? Who did he think would help him? How does this work? How does it work that a planter takes on apparently magical powers? What are people actually experiencing when they look at the planter? Do different people experience different things? And what could possibly be the relationship to those refund checks from the insurance company?

He walked and questioned. He looked at vendors selling hot dogs and old people at bus stops. He watched pigeons pick at food dropped on the street. As he remembered his Buddhist training, he remembered his oneness with all he saw and took a deep breath.

Had he driven to Charlotte on a wild goose chase? Was there nothing here to connect him to the next step, whatever it might be? How do you say to an old woman at a bus stop that there is a planter 75 miles to the west that could make her feel like she could do anything, even sit at a bus stop with a little more love for life?

And was that what the planter offered, love for life? Had he learned in his weeks of sitting next to the planter, his time of watching other people approach and stand in awe, that the key to happiness or a deep sense of fulfillment is simply to love life? Am I to simply treat life like a lover, to feel and act on a profound sense of love for even the mundane and the maddening aspects of ordinary existence? Was that it? Was that what all this had meant?

His cell phone rang in its holster on his belt. He punched the answer button and said, "This is Russell Cambry."

The voice on the other end said, "Mr. Cambry, my name is Averill Lumkin. I work for Consistent Life Insurance. I'd like to talk with you about this planter and the refund you received from our company."

Cambry could scarcely believe his ears.

"Mr. Cambry, are you there?"

"Yes, yes I am, Mr . . . . I'm sorry. I didn't catch your name," Russell Cambry said.

"It's Averill Lumkin, sir. I work for Consistent . . ."

"I heard you say whom you work for. I just am somewhat startled by this phone call. I was just thinking about your insurance company, and you call me. That's a bit unnerving," Cambry said.

"Would you prefer I call at another time?" Lumkin said.

"Oh God, no. These sorts of things don't happen every day. Your timing is perfect. How may I help you?" Cambry asked.

"I'm at the Charlotte Douglas airport. I plan to rent a car today and drive to Rutherfordton, and you're one of the people on my list to meet. I understand you are very actively promoting this planter at great personal expense to yourself," Lumkin said.

"No need to rent a car, Mr. Lumkin. I'll pick you up at the airport," Cambry said.

"Oh, don't bother, sir," Lumkin insisted.

"No, you don't bother, Mr. Lumkin. For some damn reason, I happen to be in Charlotte today, and until I received your phone call, I wasn't exactly sure why. Now, I think I know although please don't ask me to explain, because I can't. I'll tell you more when we meet."

They arranged to meet, and within the hour they were driving back to Rutherfordton, back to the planter.

After a few words of greeting, they began the gentle art of question and answer.

"Do you know a man named Rudy Dudley?" Lumpkin asked the Buddhist rich man, hoping to establish a relationship between Cambry and the software engineer who lifted more than six million dollars from his company.

"No, should I?" the Buddhist answered.

"Not necessarily."

"Is he involved in the distribution of the refund checks?" the Buddhist asked.

"Perhaps," Lumkin answered, not sure that he should reveal any details of the check scandal to this stranger, although clearly Russell Cambry had quite a stake in the planter and these people who were gathering around it, some of whom had received the refund checks.

Cambry glanced over at Lumkin while concentrating primarily on his driving. Clearly Lumkin was looking for this Rudy Dudley. If Dudley had nothing to do with the checks, Lumkin would not have asked about him.

"How can I help you, Mr. Lumkin?" Cambry decided to let Lumkin control the conversation since Lumkin appeared unwilling to reveal much information on his own.

Lumkin, on the other hand, was at a loss as to how to proceed. If Cambry knew Dudley and simply chose to hide him, Lumkin figured eventually that would come out. However if Cambry didn't know Dudley, he couldn't decide the next question.

"You're sure you don't know Rudy Dudley?" Lumkin asked again.

Cambry decided to play coy, perhaps fish out Lumkin's reason for giving so little information.

"Is he someone I would have known in college or maybe a former customer? I've been retired for several years now, and many of my casual acquaintances have faded from memory."

Lumkin hated to give anything away, but he chanced it, "You would have had contact with him much more recently."

Cambry let the car speed along at just over 75 miles per hour still being passed by many of the drivers on Interstate 85 between Charlotte and Kings Mountain.

"Could he have gone by another name?" Cambry asked and was delighted to hear Lumkin take a quick breath at the question. Maybe that meant he could have gone by another name.

Both men rode along in silence before Lumkin spoke again.

"Dudley Dumpling."

Cambry drew a quick breath this time, an old technique he had learned for controlling laughter. Had he not had experience with complex business negotiations, which held opportunities for explosive laughter at surprising trivia, he would have laughed very long and hard at Dudley Dumpling.

Still he had never met or heard of anyone by such a bizarre name.

Chapter Eight

CAROL TANIC LISTED HER HUSBAND and her son, as the two people she had wronged most deeply with her addiction to Oxycotton.

She took out a yellow legal pad and wrote with a blue Bic pen, "Pain, betrayal, lies, creepiness, ugliness, crap, dirty hands, crust, crushed, heartache, stupidity, nonsense, roughness, crap again, impurity, filth, anger, scratches (it made her think of fingernails scratching a black board,) vomit, puke, punches, more pain, more sense of senselessness, despair, hopelessness, cross, crossing, death, despair again, death again, don't commit suicide."

She knew how she would make amends to her son. She would spend as much time as she could with him, love him, laugh with him, take him places, listen to him talk, ask him questions, "be there" in the strange nomenclature of divorce, be as present as possible as often as possible, at least until he hit those teen years when she would be the most boring person alive, a crusty old mother hanging around like a stain on the wall or a piece of pottery, cracked but you hate to throw it away.

Until she became cracked pottery, she would spend as much time as possible with her son.

Mac Hartwell's cat had meowed at least a dozen times. God, he suddenly realized he had no idea how many times the cat had meowed. He pulled himself out of his favorite chair, and reached for the can opener. His arms and legs felt heavy. He listened to himself sighing, almost as though the person sighing were someone else. He looked over at his picture of Simone Weil and remembered that many people saw her death by malnutrition as a suicide.

"No danger of that," Mac mumbled to himself as he looked at the boxes of mac and cheese on his kitchen shelves and remembered how he hoped to lose weigh at some point in his life, once he . . . the cat meowing interrupted his thinking.

"Yes, Dear One, I'm coming."

He filled the cat's bowl. He set the food in front of the cat. He moved back to his favorite chair. He thought, "I'm depressed." He thought about the planter. He looked around and saw his car keys. He thought, "I can drive there in an hour." So he did.

And he stood in the yard in front of the planter and looked around. Other people were coming and going. The security guards Russell Cambry had hired stood around the parking lot Cambry had paid for and around the double-wide trailer where the Crenshaws still were trying to live a relatively normal life. He looked at the people looking at the planter. One woman wept quietly as she leaned back in her lawn chair and folded her hands in her lap. Most of the people either sat in lawn furniture or stood holding each other and smiling at the planter.

Lisa Crenshaw, the little girl, walked up to Mac and asked him, "Why aren't you looking at the planter?"

"I'm looking at the people," Mac said.

"How does that feel to you?" she asked.

"I don't feel too much of anything. I'm depressed," he said.

"What is that like?" she said.

"It is a heaviness, a feeling of being pulled into my center, as if my insides were a huge bathtub being drained down into the center of the earth," he said. "It makes me very tired." He looked at the little girl as though he were in the presence of an angel or a Hollywood alien.

"Where do you think that feeling came from?" she asked.

"I'm not sure I am a citizen of this planet," he said and smiled as if to hint that he might be kidding, but also to let her know if she planned flying off to some distant star, he'd like to hitch a ride.

"You don't feel comfortable here? You don't feel like you belong?" she asked.

"That would be one way of putting it," he said.

"Why don't you look at the planter?" she asked.

He did, and he felt better.

"How is that possible?" he asked. "I came down here because I knew it would make me feel better, but it doesn't seem possible."

"The Bible says with God all things are possible," Lisa said and folded her arms of front of her and starting looking at the planter and feeling better, too.

"Yes, but, I don't think many people have thought that would have a practical application. It's not the kind of thought that most people think works very practically. It's more like a myth or a fairy tale," Mac said.

"But aren't all myths, fairy tales, all those kinds of things supposed to be full of meaning and power?" Lisa asked.

"Well, yes, but you just never figure something like this to actually happen," Mac said and looked back at the planter and felt better again. "It's very, very strange."

"Mama is fine with it, but it's driving Daddy insane. I just wish he would accept things as they are," Lisa said.

"Isn't that one of the hardest lessons we have to learn in life?" Mac asked the little girl.

"It isn't for me," Lisa said as if it were the most obvious thing in the world.

"Do they sell ice cream up at that concession stand that Mr. Cambry built?" Mac asked.

"Yes, they do," Lisa reported.

"Do you think your Mama and Daddy would mind if I bought you some ice cream?" Mac asked.

"Well, since they can see that concession stand from the front window and keep an eye on me, I guess they would think it was all right, but let's go get permission just in case," Lisa suggested.

Mary and Billy Ray were discussing the planter for the umpteenth time.

"They're never going away, Mary," her husband told her, and he said it as though he believed she could make them go away.

"And if they don't?" she asked looking up from a pie crust she was pinching the edges on while Billy Ray cradled an afternoon cup of coffee.

"Lisa has no chance at a normal childhood with the front yard full of strangers morning, noon and night," Billy Ray complained.

"Since when has Lisa Crenshaw been a normal child? She was telling us about Jesus when she three years old. We've had her examined by a psychiatrist, who says there is absolutely nothing wrong with her," Mary spoke calmly, but took several deep breaths as she continued to pinch the edges of her pie crust.

"That was before all this, baby," Billy Ray insisted and shifted in his kitchen chair like a man on trial.

"And how is this making her different?" Mary asked continuing to draw long breaths through her nose.

"Mary, for Pete's sake. Will you be reasonable?"

"What do you want me to do, Billy Ray?" Mary held her calm, reasonable tone. "Do you want me to tell Russell Cambry to keep his money? Do you want me to tell Lisa that she could have gone to college, but her Daddy didn't want strangers standing in the front yard when clearly something very spiritual is going on?" Mary asked.

"Just exactly what is the spiritual thing that is going on, Mary?" Billy Ray asked raising his volume and tempo just a tad.

"You know perfectly well that I have no idea, Billy Ray Crenshaw. But I know it feels like a miracle, like an appearance of the Virgin Mary like happened over in Yugoslavia or down in Mexico. It feels like 50,000 people showing up for a Billy Graham crusade. It feels like a miracle, but I don't know what it is. I just know Russell Cambry is enough impressed with it that he got us out of debt, set Lisa up to go to college, and that puts us about a quarter million dollars ahead of the rest of the people in this neighborhood, and I, for one, am mighty grateful," she said upping her volume and tempo just a tad as she poured the pie filling into the shell.

"He's a Buddhist for Pete's Sake, Mary," Billy Ray continued to whine.

"His money spends just like a Baptist's, and there's not a Baptist within a thousand miles of here willing to put our daughter through college," she clipped the words like grass flying from a lawn mower as she started crossing the top of her pie with strips of dough.

"Mama, Daddy, ya'll remember Mr. Mac Hartwell. He came down from Marion a few weeks ago to look at the planter," Lisa said as she walked into the kitchen with Mac on her heels.

"Sorry for the interruption, folks," Mac said.

"Oh, we're used to it," Billy Ray practically snarled.

"My husband is a bit irritated at the moment, Mr. Hartwell. He is not usually rude," Mary said wiping her hands on a towel and reaching to shake Mac's.

"Don't embarrass me in front of strangers, Mary," Billy Ray said without yelling or scolding, and Mary heard the seriousness in his voice. She stopped dead in her tracks and turned to face her husband.

"You're right, Billy Ray. I believe I was the one being rude," she said without the first hint of sarcasm.

"Maybe I should come back at another time," Mac offered and turned to leave.

"Mr. Hartwell offered to buy me an ice cream over at the concession stand," Lisa said in hopes of keeping Mac from leaving.

Neither of her parents spoke for a moment. Billy Ray felt this was exactly the kind of disaster that might scar Lisa for life. Mary sensed that Mac was okay, but each was watching the other for a reaction. Mac sensed he really ought to leave.

But he surprised himself.

"Your daughter is extraordinary," Mac began.

"We know," Billy Ray said.

"Please," Mary begged.

"I, on the other hand, am not. Many of my friends think I'm crazy because I have a hard time fitting in wherever I work, but other than that, I live a pretty humdrum life. No, let me put that another way. I live the kind of life nobody would notice. I read. I enjoy movies and friends and my cat, but I struggle to fit in almost anywhere I go, whomever I hang out with. Your extraordinary daughter has made me feel like that's okay. She makes me feel like it is okay to not be so okay. I realize that really doesn't make a lot of sense, but I'd just like to show my gratitude by sharing some ice cream with her. I certainly understand if you'd prefer not," Mac said quietly.

"Why don't I come along?" Billy Ray offered.

"That would be delightful," Mac said. The tension in the room was gone.

"I've got a pie in the oven, or I'd come, too," Mary offered and looked at her husband to say a silent, "Thank you."

The concession stand is just that, a small trailer with picnic tables arranged nearby. Mac paid for three cones. He had mint chocolate chip. Lisa had vanilla, and Billy Ray had strawberry.

"I've never understood people eating vanilla ice cream. I think it's delicious, but when there are so many choices," Mac wondered as they gathered around one of the picnic tables.

"I don't always get it," Lisa said and smiled.

"But it's your favorite," Billy Ray teased.

"Not always," Lisa retorted.

"Emerson said, 'A foolish consistency is the hobgoblin of small minds,'" Mac quoted.

"Tell me what that means, Mr. Hartwell," Lisa asked.

"It probably means different things to different people," Mac admitted. "But to me it means don't always take the same way to work or school, don't always part your hair the same way, and for the love of all that's holy, don't always eat the same flavor of ice cream. You can bore yourself to death with consistency," Mac explained.

"I always eat strawberry," Billy Ray said and twisted his mouth to one side as he worried he was in dangerous territory.

"You are not boring, Daddy. I'm sure many fascinating people always eat strawberry," Lisa piped in rescuing her father. "And I also think people take different steps in following Jesus."

This path in the conversation did not appeal to Mac, because he had left the Nazarene behind many years before. He found Christians to be insufferable, and Christianity to be much too constricting.

Lisa was not deterred by the silence of either of the grown men who sat across from her at the picnic table.

"Some people have deeply emotional experiences of Jesus because they see him as the most important person who ever lived and they are so grateful that he saved the world," the little girl said. "Other people just see him as the guy whose picture is hanging on the wall at church; and they never think about him much except on Sunday morning and even then very little."

"And you?" Mac asked. "How do you see Jesus?"

"He is very much like you. He has unlimited potential. He is capable of absolutely anything."

"You can't think Mr. Hartwell and Jesus are the same, Lisa," Billy Ray scolded.

"The Gospel of John says so, Daddy. It says Jesus dwells in the Father and in us, and he says the believers will do even greater things than he has done," Lisa argued.

"But Jesus was the savior," Billy Ray argued.

"I know," Lisa agreed and licked her vanilla cone.

"Mr. Hartwell ain't nobody's savior," Billy said and grinned at Mac.

Lisa looked at both of the grown ups, took another lick, and said, "He saves himself every day. He eats, he sleeps, he keeps himself relatively safe. He lives in the mountains, but doesn't drive off the sides of any of them, and when he gets the chance, he loves other people. That's what the Bible says do," Lisa said without betraying too much of her exasperation with having to deal with her Daddy, a man who did not share her sense of the way things are. Sometimes Billy wished that child would hush.

"But Jesus died for him," Billy Ray soldiered on, not realizing he was outgunned in a very unfair fight.

"And I'm sure, given the chance, Mr. Hartwell would die for Jesus," Lisa quipped.

"Oh, I'm not sure about that at all'" Mac said. "I know many people have died for their faith. But, Lisa, in all fairness, I have to tell you. I'm not even a follower of Jesus," Mac admitted.

"Oh, my Lord," Billy Ray uttered and look at Mac as though he'd just crapped his pants.

"Well, of course you are," Lisa shook her head and took a big lick from her ice cream. Billy Ray and Mac were working their cones pretty hard, too. "You don't have to claim to be a follower of Jesus to be a follower of Jesus. In fact, Jesus told a story to illustrate the point. He said a father had two sons whom he asked to go into the vineyard and work. One said he would but didn't. The other said he wouldn't but did. Which one had the father's favor?"

"What in the world does that mean?" Billy Ray grumbled.

"Come on, Daddy. It's obvious. Jesus isn't interested in people saying they will love their neighbors and pray for their enemies and make peace and feed hungry children. He's interested in people who do it. Mr. Hartwell is following Jesus every time he is kind to his cat," Lisa said.

"How do you know I have a cat?" Mac asked.

"I mean if you have a cat," she said and tipped her head to one side so as to say, "No big deal."

"You cannot deny Jesus before men. I know enough Bible to know that," Billy Ray grumbled even more, started to feel about Lisa as he always had, that she was about to get on his last nerve with all her philosophies.

"But ultimately nobody denies Jesus, Daddy. The smallest act of kindness, even bringing a cup of cold water to anyone who serves God is enough to show that you understand how much God loves you and how you are a servant of God," Lisa countered.

"Where in the world did you hear that?" Billy Ray worked his mouth like he might explode at any moment.

"The tenth chapter of Matthew," she said softly and kept licking her vanilla.

Carol Tanic did spend time with her son, Jake. It was not easy. Like many divorced parents, especially those without custody, she was wildly indulgent, spending more money than she should on video games on movies, giving up huge chunks of time to watching movies with him that sometime made her cringe at the violence and sex, but offering him as much unconditional love, affirmation, support, and indulgence as she could muster. But she believed, at the core of her being, that he was the most wonderful creature alive.

Sometimes she would say it, "Jake, you are the most wonderful creature alive."

Sometimes he would just lap it up with a big grin. "Thanks, Mom. You're not so bad yourself."

When she applied for her job with Rutherford Weekly, Jake was with her. Because of a mix up over child care, Jake sat in a back room at the publication's offices in Rutherfordton and overheard his mother say, "I will work very hard at this job, but you have to understand my son is my number one priority."

Walking away from the meeting, Jake asked, "You told that man in there that I'm your number one priority. Is that right?"

"Of course you are, darling," she said and threw her arms around him.

They held each other in the parking lot and squeezed each other for just a moment. Carol felt her heart exploding in her chest.

As they walked on to the car, Jake asked, "Are you a drug addict, Mom?"

"I'm a recovering drug addict, which is why I don't get to live in the same house with you, but it means I've got the drugs out of my life and I get to hug you in parking lots and movie houses and places where they rent video games," Carol said.

"Speaking of," Jake said.

"The game room is our next stop, Mr. Wonderful," Carol said.

"Thanks, Mom," Jake said.

Carol and Jake once heard a story-teller named Kathryn Wyndom from Mobile, Alabama. She was speaking at the National Storytelling Festival in Jonesboro, TN. Ms. Wyndom was 91 years old and stood at a microphone for an hour and told stories of her childhood, her college days, her life in general with a humor and grace that left Carol weeping tears of joy.

The line that tore Carol's heart into a star burst of joy was when she quoted from a poem she hopes is read at her funeral.

"She was twice blessed. She was happy and she knew it."

For Carol Tanic, a divorced recovering drug addict, drinking deep from a beautiful October afternoon in the presence of the most wonderful creature alive, that line was more than she could process and maintain her composure. In the midst of an audience of a thousand listeners, she started to heave like she might rupture and wail like she'd just lost a favorite dog.

She kept on crying as they exited the event. Jake walked along beside her hoping she might stop. He said, "Mom, you're still crying."

With her nose running and her eyes bulging out of her head like tomatoes, she choked out, "I know, honey. I'm almost done."

Another hundred yards or so, almost to their car, Carol called a dear friend from years past, her old telephone buddy, Mac Hartwell. Mac was off in the woods with his cat, so Carol got Mac's answering machine. This is the message she left, "Mac, I'm climbing a hill on the most gorgeous October afternoon, watching leaves blow between me and Jake. I have just heard the most heart-warming line of poetry I think I ever heard in my life, which I'll tell you about later, and I am looking at the most beautiful 11-year-old boy on the face of the earth."

A few hours later, after returning Jake to his father's house, always a heart-breaking moment, although it got easier with time, Carol called Jake to tell him goodnight.

"Mom, what was your favorite part of the weekend?"

Carol recounted a couple of other story tellers they had heard, and then quoted again that line from that poem, "She was twice blessed. She was happy and she knew it."

Jake said, "My favorite part was when you called your friend and told him I was the most beautiful 11-year-old boy in the whole world."

They cried together over the telephone, a broken-hearted mom and a broken-hearted son winding together the chords of their love through the keening of their grief and the consolation they drew from how much they sounded alike.

As part of her spiritual journey, Carol Tanic, an atheist who loves Jesus, had sat in Buddhist meditation. Among the people to whom she sold advertising, many of whom were fundamentalist Christians, such a practice would make no sense. But for her it was a way of dealing with the grief of losing daily contact with her son, Jake, a little boy whose pain felt to her so much greater than even his body or his soul. although she thought that was a crazy thought, too. How could anything be larger than our souls? Still, as she remembered crying with Jake on the phone, she thought his pain might well be larger than his soul.

"It's very hard for you, isn't it, Daddy?" Lisa Crenshaw asked her daddy, Billy Ray.

"You mean being in this freak show?" he asked her as she snuggled down for another night's sleep, and he tucked her in bed.

"If you have to call it that, yes, that's what I mean," she said, and gazed into his eyes out of her beautiful freckled face, a face he believed was as beautiful as any he had ever seen, yes, even maybe more beautiful than her mother's.

"You know it's hard for me," he said and stood by her bed remembering the many times she had started conversations like this, remembering she was about to blow his mind again with some pearl of wisdom.

"Do you think people ever choose the hard stuff in their lives, Daddy?"

"That makes no sense to me, Lisa," he said, and he knew he was just being honest.

"Is it possible that deep down inside you, there was a little something that wanted what you call this freak show?" she asked.

"Oh, baby," he sat on the edge of her bed and looked around at her room. Just over her white princess dresser, with the Noah's Ark lamp and lamp shade, a picture of the chestnut-haired Jesus hung. It was one of those head and shoulder shots that Jesus apparently posed for dozens of times, because there are so many of them in homes and Sunday School classrooms all over the Baptist Southland. Some strange source of light came from behind his head, and he smiled into the camera as if to assure us all, everything is going to be all right. On the other side of the room, Mary had hung another common image of the carpenter from Nazareth, a shepherd's staff in one hand, a gaggle of children gathered around looking up at him as they knew what the grown ups had clearly missed, this guy had something very, very special.

"I just can't figure why I would have wanted all this to happen," Billy Ray finally said after looking around at the decorations in his daughter's room.

"Maybe you wanted to know God better," Lisa said.

"But why, baby?" he said to her at a deep place, talking with her as he would talk with no one else in his life, including his wife. "God's in the church, ain't he? Ain't God in the Sunday School classes and the eleven o'clock service? Ain't God in the hymns and the prayers and the sermons even if the sermons do sometimes sound a lot alike?"

"Maybe it wasn't enough," Lisa suggested.

"It has always bothered me that people can be such hypocrites. You know, how a man can teach Sunday School for 20 years and still be mean to his wife? I mean, you know, how can God let a man get that close to the truth and still not get through to him? Do you get where I'm coming from?" he asked his daughter.

"Sure, Daddy," Lisa said.

"But this planter, is it from God or the devil?" Billy Ray asked.

"There ain't no devil, Daddy," Lisa offered.

He shifted on her mattress so he could see her better and scolded, "Hush your mouth, baby girl. The Bible says there's a devil, so there has to be one."

"Everything in the Bible ain't real, Daddy. You remember when Jesus told that story about the Good Samaritan?" Lisa asked.

"Sure, everybody knows that story," Billy Ray said.

"Well, it's just a story. It didn't really happen. Jesus just told a story to make a point. It didn't really happen," she said.

"Yeah, but the devil, he's over in the part that did happen," Billy Ray insisted.

"Jesus said most of the evil men do comes out of themselves. That's what ought to be worrying us more than any devil," she said and sighed as if to say, "This is sure a lot of work."

"You are so smart, little girl, but you are still just a little girl. You know, even Jesus waited until he was 30 before he started his ministry," Billy Ray said.

"You think I ought to wait before I start thinking about things, Daddy?" she asked.

"I think sometimes you think too much," her Daddy said. "I reckon you better get some sleep."

Once he crawled into bed with Mary, she said, "That sounded like a big talk."

"She thinks there is something down inside of me that wanted this planter to show up so I'd have more God in my life," he told her as he felt the familiar softness of the pillow fold around his head.

"And maybe she's right?" Mary asked in that deep alto voice that had made him love her so in the first place.

"I know I'm supposed to love God with all of my heart, but sometimes I just want to watch TV and forget about everything, and that does not feel like loving God with all my heart," he admitted.

"It would be nice if every problem in the world could be solved by Walker Texas Ranger, wouldn't it?" she asked and draped her arm across his chest.

"You know it," he agreed.

"You better kiss me goodnight, Billy Ray," she murmured, and he did.

Outside their double-wide home on the side of a mountain a security guard hired by Russell Cambry kept watch. A full moon shown on the parking lot, the concession stand, the picnic tables, the port-a-johns, and the planter. A web cam sent the images through the Internet to anyone who wanted to take a look.

Chapter Nine

RUSSELL CAMBRY DECIDED TO USE another tact with Averill Lumkin since neither man had revealed much to the other.

"Let me just speculate a little here, Mr. Lumkin. I received a refund check from your company. Most insurance companies don't just randomly send out checks, especially not to dozens of people, maybe many more. We know of several dozen who have received the checks and come to look at the planter. Some of them have even begun meeting together to try to figure out what it all means," Cambry said.

"Meeting together?" Lumkin seemed startled by the news.

"Yes," Cambry answered and hoped Lumkin would say more, but he continued with the silence of a poker player. So Cambry kept speculating. "They have learned they have in common a civic spirit. Most of them volunteer for some kind of nonprofit organization. They work with women who are in violent relationships with their husbands or boyfriends, volunteer fire departments, garden clubs, community theaters and environmental groups, libraries, and glee clubs. You get the picture."

Lumkin himself belonged to a stamp collecting group in Omaha. He wondered if that was the same kind of group Cambry was describing.

Again Cambry paused in hopes Lumkin would join in with some feedback. Nothing, so far.

"There is even a Hollywood TV producer who is optioning a show about the planter and the people who have been touched by it," Cambry said.

"Oh dear," Lumkin uttered and immediately wished he had not.

"That alarms you?" Cambry asked.

"Surely they would not involve the company," Lumkin hoped.

"I don't see how it could be avoided," Cambry said, and felt certain this would open his recalcitrant companion to a little more conversation.

"Why not?" Lumkin ventured.

"Well, all these people received refund checks from your company. It is that remarkable coincidence, if you believe in coincidences, that has brought them together. The planter is surely a factor, but the checks are something of a remarkable common denominator," Cambry chatted casually as if he were describing the art of watching paint dry.

"How is that possible?" Lumkin practically groaned.

"Maybe Rudy Dudley could explain it," Cambry offered.

Lumkin simply looked at Cambry, and Cambry looked away from the traffic long enough to meet his gaze and look back at the traffic. The Buddhist said nothing, but waited for the insurance executive to speak. After a few seconds he did speak.

"I am operating under that assumption, but I can't find him. He moved to Thailand several years ago, and no one there seems to know what became of him. He wrote the software that paid these refund checks before leaving our company. We have no idea why. We've corrected the software, but we want to talk to him, possibly prosecute him and have him put in prison," Lumkin said with resignation. He knew he had let the cat out of the bag to Cambry, but felt finally he could trust him.

"What was the damage?" Cambry asked softly.

"Over six million dollars, more than 26,000 checks," Lumkin barely spoke.

"So I need to build a parking lot for 26,000 people to visit the planter?" Cambry asked more to himself than Lumkin.

"I beg your pardon?" Lumkin asked.

"Oh, nothing," Cambry said, but felt deeply, it was something, and therefore it could not be nothing. He also thought that mountainside where the Crenshaws lived could not accommodate 26,000 people.

The meetings had long ago outgrown the back room of Aunt Sally's restaurant in Polkville.

Miz Whisnant had negotiated with her church to use the fellowship hall, but even it was starting to feel crowded as the most recent gathering had topped 100 participants.

"We have a motion on the floor that we support the King David hospital for the treatment of malnutrition in Port O Prince, Haiti. They have requested $10,000," Miz Whisnant intoned with her rich voice.

"And we have witnesses who can account for their effective use of these funds?" one sister asked from the floor.

"Goes without saying, Sister Alice. Nothing makes it to the floor without our doing a thorough check first. Is this your first meeting with this group?" Miz Whisnant kidded gently.

"It is," Sister Alice answered to the soft laughter of those near her.

"All is forgiven," Miz Whisnant added.

The motion passed easily.

"Now, where is the money coming from? Is anyone comfortable with taking the whole load?" she asked with a big grin.

"I believe the spirit is moving Sister Alice to write that check," somebody piped in from the back of the room.

"Lord God," Sister Alice sounded like she had been shot.

"Hold on, dear. That was a joke," Miz Whisnant held out her arms like she might catch the sister should she faint.

"You better believe it was a joke," Sister Alice stood and looked back across the room like she might want to hit somebody.

"Can anybody go $5,000?" Miz Whisnant asked ignoring the standing sister, who then sat.

"Over here," a voice spoke and a hand shot up. Applause rippled through the crowd.

"If you gonna clap for five thousand, you better clap for five, because we will be there soon," Miz Whisnant encouraged, and the incremental giving moved down through the thousands and hundreds until the total was hit. Checks were passed to the front, and those in attendance were again amazed at the efficiency of the system.

Before the night was over, three other requests were granted for a total of over $30,000. Newcomers looked on in slack-jawed surprise. Folks who had been coming for weeks just smiled at each other. Noticing the look of shock on so many faces around the room, Miz Whisnant offered a phrase that had become common, "The planter has convinced us that healing the planet is no big deal."

"Miz Whisnant," Jenifer Davis, the reporter for The Daily Courier stood.

"Yes, Miz Davis?" she recognized the reporter.

"Is the planet going to be healed in increments of $30,000? And if so, isn't it going to take a very long time?" she asked.

"We trust the process, Miz Davis. We don't know much about how long anything is going to take, but we do the good we can in the time allotted." A murmur of agreement trickled around the room.

"Aren't thousands dying of hunger in Haiti while this hospital is only able to save a few?" the reporter asked insistently.

The crowd was not happy with her questions and this time the murmur sounded angry.

"Hold your peace, brothers and sisters. Her job is to ask hard questions. Miz Davis, we have felt empowered by our experience of the planter to do more than we have done in other areas of our lives. We don't understand it, but we like it. It had made us feel good. There are just over a hundred people in this room tonight. We are in the process of finding bigger rooms, because our numbers keep growing, but we have no illusions that we can solve all the problems of the world. Some problems will always be with us, but we can do what we can in the time allotted. The planter has simply raised our expectations of what we can do."

"And will you be able to sustain your efforts, as noble as they are? What you accomplished tonight feels remarkable," Jenfier said.

"It feels that way to us, too," Miz Whisnant agreed, and the crowd signaled its approval with laughter and applause.

"So will you be able to keep it up?" Jenifer asked again.

"It feels very good to think so," Miz Whisnant answered and again received the warm support of the gathering. "Miz Davis, if you will forgive me, we have one more item of business. I call on my beloved sister, Carol Tanic, for an announcement."

Carol stood and looked out on the crowd. She could hardly believe her eyes. Black, brown, and white faces looked back at her. She knew most of the people present and knew they were rich and poor, educated and not so educated, Jewish, Hindu, yes even in Western North Carolina, Catholic and Protestant, and of course, at least one Buddhist, Russell Cambry, looked back at her.

"We have reached an agreement with Rutherfordton United Methodist Church to begin meeting in their fellowship hall. This meeting will continue here thanks to the generosity of Miz Whisnant's church. We are also negotiating with motels, community centers, and fire departments in other towns. Our numbers are growing to the point we cannot continue to hold our gatherings to one location. Thank you all for your support, and continue to encourage your friends to either visit the planter or take a look at it on the web site," Carol said and sat down. Her heart beat in her chest at a high rate. She was beside herself with joy and took long deep breaths to contain her emotions.

She reached over to the chair beside her and squeezed Mac Hartwell's hand. The room erupted in applause and cheering.

When Lumkin saw the planter, he could scarcely believe his heart. He felt so good he didn't recognize the feeling. A lifetime of suppressing almost every feeling had frozen him pretty deeply. He had lived in an emotional Thermos jug, where every doubt, every passion, every fear, and especially every wave of anger had to be quick frozen and dropped into an underground freezer where colon cancer waited to thaw it all out years later down the road.

"What is this?" he allowed himself to wonder, but he also looked quickly away.

"Most people like to look at it, Mr. Lumkin," Lisa said to the insurance executive. The two had just been introduced by Russell Cambry, as had her parents. Lumkin only smiled at Lisa and looked at the other adults as through the conversation would surely move along.

"She's right, Mr. Lumkin," Mary said, noticing the pinched-face accountant looked like he might need to use the bathroom. Lumkin said nothing, so Mary pushed it. "Don't you like looking at the planter?"

"I didn't come here for that," he said.

"It's free, Mr. Lumkin. All you have to do is look," Lisa said.

"What a curious little girl you are," Lumkin said.

"You're not the first to notice that," Billy Ray inserted.

"Give it a another look, Mr. Lumkin. You looked away awfully fast last time," Lisa noticed.

"I'm a little bit busy, young lady," Lumkin insisted.

"And that causes so many problems, Mr. Lumkin," Lisa urged and pointed at the planter.

Lumkin worked his mouth to signal his surrender, but he hesitated before turning back to take that second look. He remained silent, the fruit of years of training. There was simply no containing his reaction. Inside where no one could see, a small volcano of joy and pleasure was erupting.

"It makes no sense," he finally admitted, "but it does feel very, very good to look at it. No wonder so many people have come."

He looked around at the Crenshaws' yard, the concession stand, the picnic tables, the extra parking lot Russell had built. About 30 people were scattered in lawn chairs, on sleeping bags, simply standing with their arms crossed, staring at the planter and grinning like someone had just given them a deep sense of personal power, joy, pleasure, fun, something amazing and wild and nonsensical.

"How is this possible?" he asked.

"That's what we're all trying to figure out," Russell Cambry said.

Mary invited everyone inside where she had fixed oatmeal raisin cookies and coffee. Lisa was served milk. The Crenshaws, Russell, and Lumkin gathered around the kitchen table.

Lumkin explained he was looking for Rudy Dudley.

Mary and Billy Ray looked at each other and shrugged.

"Never heard of him," Billy Ray said.

"Does he make planters?" Mary asked and smiled.

Lumkin didn't answer. He drummed his fingers on the kitchen table and looked around. He recounted for Mary, Lisa, and Billy Ray what he had told Russell in the car, how Dudley had written the software that sent six million dollars out to 26,000 people in the mountains of Virginia and the Carolinas.

"Twenty six thousand?" Billy Ray gasped and looked at Russell.

"I know, I know. We can't accommodate them all," Russell said and shook his head.

"You believe they'll all come here?" Lumkin asked, his curiosity piqued as it had rarely been.

"Over two thousand have come. Hundreds are attending meetings to figure out how we can work together to make a better world," Russell explained. "Every time someone comes here to look at the Planter, we ask them if they received a refund check. We're creating a data base and staying in touch with each other."

"Make a better world?" Lumkin asked wondering if he had not fallen with Alice down the rabbit hole.

"Feed the hungry, create peace between historically warring groups, provide basic medical care and education to low-income populations, you know social justice work," Russell said casually. Lumkin thought about what he had just heard. He knew there were people like this in the world, because he had seen news stories about things like this. He knew Bill and Melinda Gates and Warren Buffet were working very hard to give lots of money away. But it was hard for him to imagine hundreds of ordinary people gathering in small towns and rural communities. It was hard for him to imagine that they could imagine themselves making a difference.

The family had fallen into a routine in the weeks since the planter had changed their lives forever. As much as they could, they held to homework, a little TV before bedtime, an occasional bowl of ice cream just before brushing teeth. Evening prayers were as normal as could be expected with Mary thanking the Lord for the blessings of their lives and Lisa adding in all the soldiers in the war, all the little children who didn't have enough to eat and the sick and the lonely. Mother and daughter would also go outside most evenings, even as summer had given way to fall and winter approached, they went out to say good night to the few stragglers who hung on from the day's viewing of the planter, to tell the evening's security guard good-night, and to look at the planter themselves one last time before the evening's rest.

Often one or the other of them would say, "It sure is beautiful. Don't you think so?"

To which the other would say, "It sure is."

On the night Averill Lumkin checked into the Carriage Houses Bed and Breakfast in downtown Rutherfordton, Lisa faked sleep and waited after hearing her daddy close the bedroom door. She threw off her bed clothes and sat on the edge of her single mattress.

"I need help," she barely whispered into the semi-darkness of her room. A security light outside her window had been blocked by a thin shade, but it still threw shadows all about.

She waited. An angel appeared before her on the edge of her dresser, eight inches high, female in features, blonde, beautiful, as if any of them could be anything but Hollywood good-looking.

She spoke with her mind, "What do you need?"

Lisa answered with thoughts rather than words, "You know what I need."

"You have the information about Rudy Dudley," the angel answered.

"I guess I knew that," Lisa replied.

"How can I help?" the angel asked.

"What do I do with what I know?" Lisa asked.

"Why not just tell the grownups and let them decide what to do?" the angel asked.

"Can they be trusted?" Lisa asked.

"They're doing pretty well so far. They're raising money for hospitals and schools all over the world. They're getting together and learning how to work together to make a better world," the angel gestured with her right hand while shrugging her approval.

"Will they believe me?" Lisa asked.

"I suppose so. They have done remarkably well so far. But who knows? I mean I thought you could predict the future," the angel said.

"In general ways I can," Lisa thought and tipped her head to one side in thought. "I know how all this will end, but particular details are hard to predict. After all the present is enough to keep up with. The future can get a little out of control if you know what I mean," Lisa said.

"Oh, I do know what you mean," the angel nodded.

"Will he go to prison if they find him?" Lisa asked.

"The insurance company people want to put him in prison," the angel acknowledged something they both already knew.

Lisa smiled.

"No prison could hold him," she thought so that the angel could hear her and grinned.

"Of course not," the angel agreed and grinned, too.

W. Dixon Franklin, the television preacher and Bible teacher sat on the other side of the planter from Russell Cambry, the Buddhist millionaire.

"The place can't hold 26,000 people," Franklin repeated something they both had said several times.

"If Lumkin doesn't give me the list of names and contact information, it could take us years to find them all anyway," Cambry mused and looked over some notes he had taken.

"If it's God's will, he'll find a way to make it happen," Franklin said and grinned like Jimmy Carter.

"But you know I don't believe in all that mumbo jumbo," Cambry said.

"Your not believing it won't make it not true," Franklin insisted.

"Good morning, gentlemen, are we any closer to solving the problems of the world?" Carol Tanic had taken a day off from work and come at the summons of Cambry by telephone the night before. The phrase, "solving the problems of the world" was one she had learned from her mother and others in that part of the country. It was usually a way rural Southerners made a little fun of each other for sitting and talking and not accomplishing a whole lot. In this case, Carol Tanic suspected a whole lot might be accomplished.

"We're plotting to convince Lumkin to give us the names of the 26,000 people who got checks," Russell said.

"Ooh, it sounds so cloak and dagger," Carol said and rubbed her palms together.

Russell just looked at her, thinking perhaps she was not taking in the gravity of the situation.

"Clearly the spirit of the Lord is on this work," W. Dixon said.

"I wish you could find some other way of expressing yourself," Russell moaned.

"It's blessed," W. Dixon insisted.

"You mean like what people say after a sneeze?" Russell asked.

Lisa had stood listening to the grown ups who showed no sign of letting up their inane banter.

"Would Mr. Lumkin tell us the names of the 26,000 people if I told him where Rudy Dudley is?" Lisa asked.

Tanic, Franklin, and Cambry all turned to the little girl.

"I think he would perhaps," Carol Tanic said.

"And what would you do with those names?" Lisa asked.

"We'd continue the work we've started. We'd work for peace, food for the world, medicine and good schools everywhere," Carol answered.

"To the glory of God," W. Dixon added.

"Or just because it's the right thing to do," Cambry said.

"You know where this Rudy Dudley is?" Carol asked.

"I know where he is, but I don't think anyone will believe me," Lisa said.

Like the cavalry in an old western, Lumkin arrived in the driveway. Miz Whisnant had picked him up from the Carriage Houses Bed and Breakfast. As he came striding across the yard, he pulled his cell phone from his pocket, held it to his ear and stopped walking. Miz Whisnant ambled on toward the deck.

"Honey, are you sure you know where Rudy Dudley is?" Carol Tanic asked.

"Good morning, everybody," Miz Whisnant chimed, but Carol held up her hand to silence the older woman.

"Honey, are you sure?" Carol repeated.

Lisa pressed her lips together.

"I'm sure nobody will believe me," Lisa said finally.

Lisa's mom, Mary, had stepped onto the deck.

"Lisa, you know we don't keep secrets in our family," Mary chided, but Lisa sighed.

"Mama, everybody keeps secrets, and honest to goodness, if I tell this one . . ."

Lumkin stepped onto the deck, and began talking without greeting anyone, "That was my office in Omaha. There's been an emergency. I need to hire a taxi or get one of you to drive me back to the airport."

"I'll do it," Russell said, stood and motioned to Carol Tanic, holding his fingers to his ear in the shape of a telephone. "Call my cell if this pans out."

"Don't worry," Carol answered, as she watched the two men walk toward Russell's car.

"What in the world is going on?" Miz Whisnant asked.

"I think young Lisa is about to tell us where she thinks Rudy Dudley is," W. Franklin said dramatically.

"Well, it's kind of a long story," Lisa said.

"Why don't we all come inside?" Mary invited. "I've got fresh coffee, and I can probably find some cookies."

In an Omaha hospital, Merrimon lay crippled by a severe heart attack. He clung to life in the hours it took Lumpkin to drive to Charlotte and fly home.

"Forget about prosecuting Rudy Dudley," Merrimon whispered to his assistant as the younger man rushed to his side. Merrimon's voice sounded strained and barely audible.

Merrimon was hooked to a series of machines that both monitored his vital signs and kept him alive.

Lumkin stood in awe of the tubes and wires that ran in every direction and filled the room with low hums and beeps.

"Forget prosecuting Dudley, sir? But he stole . . ."

"He didn't schteal . . ." Merrimon slurred the words. "It uz their money."

A nurse stepped in.

"He's really in no condition to talk," she said.

"I gotta talk . . ." Merrimon groaned.

"Just a few minutes?" Lumkin asked.

"Five minutes," the nurse backed out of the room.

"I saw him in a dream. He's okay," Merrimon could barely get the words out.

"A dream?" Lumkin asked. He understood the word, but could not understand how it could make any sense coming from this hardened corporate executive.

"Yes, please just be quiet and listen," Merrimon grunted and groaned in pain. "I'm dying, son. Bless you for all you've done for the company. But you've got to get back to North Carolina and listen to that little girl. This is the most important thing you've ever done."

"What do I ask the little girl? You mean the Crenshaw girl?"

"Yes," he said and nodded and took a breath.

"Dudley came to me in a dream. This is huge, Lumkin. Don't blow this. Death is no big deal, son. But life, oh my God. Life is huge, Lumkin. Life is where we're supposed to be doing our work," Merrimon could barely utter the words, but Lumkin was baffled by them.

"Sir, I'm sorry . . ." Lumkin tried to say how little he understood, but Merrimon waved it away.

"Be sorry for not living life, Lumkin. That's something to be sorry about. Oh, God, I am in pain, man, but you've got to promise me. Get back on the next plane to North Carolina. Talk to the little girl, the little Crenshaw girl. Dudley told me in the dream," Merrimon forced the words out.

"But, sir, he's a criminal," Lumkin insisted.

"So was Jesus, you dumb schmuck. Now go talk to that little girl," Merrimon said.

"I'm really sorry, sir," the nurse came back. Lumkin walked out of the room, and called a cab from his cell phone.

Billy Ray came in from the TV room and dragged in a couple of extra chairs. Mary served coffee to Carol, Miz Whisnant, W. Dixon, and her husband. Lisa wrapped her fingers around a tall glass of milk and stared at a plate full of cookies.

"So, honey, you wanted to tell us about Rudy Dudley?" Carol asked.

"What difference will it make if you have those names?" Lisa asked.

"Child," Miz Whisnant chimed in. "We have met with hundreds of them so far. They're good people. They're people who don't let their egos get ahead of good sense. Most of them are small town folk, caring folk, volunteers in the fire department or the church choir. Some of them are radicals like that crowd I ran with back when Dr. King was alive. We changed the world back then, honey, and if my suspicions are true, we can change it again. We got to find these people. They're people who care about immigrants and poor people, gay and lesbian people and people who make diesel fuel out of soy beans, all kinds of people who believe that what's good for everybody is eventually going to be good for everybody."

"Mr. Rudy Dudley believes you can change the world with those people," Lisa said.

"You've met him?" Mary asked. It wasn't so much a question, as it was a statement, but Mary made it sound like a question because she knew it would strain credibility for her to anticipate what was quickly becoming obvious to her if not to any of the others. Somehow Lisa had met Rudy Dudley.

"I'm still afraid you won't believe me," Lisa looked around at the grown ups.

"Tell us the truth, and we won't have any trouble believing you," W. Dixon said.

"My daughter don't lie, preacher," Billy Ray piped up.

"Very well," W. Dixon said and turned back to Lisa with his Jimmy Carter grin.

"I've met him," Lisa said.

Billy Ray wanted to say that was impossible, but he held his tongue.

"Where?"

"Here," she said.

"He's been here at this house," Mary just said it that time, did not make it into a question.

"Yes," she said.

"And?" Carol asked.

"He told me everything that was going to happen. He told me about Ms. Whisnant, Mr. W. Dixon Franklin, Ms. Tanic, all these people who have come. He knows all of you. He's been working on this for more than 20 years, collecting files, creating a data base, and working on the software for the insurance company."

"Why you, honey?" Mary asked as she blinked back tears.

"He said a little child shall lead them," Lisa said.

"Book of Isaiah," W. Dixon referred to the Hebrew prophecy.

"Same book that says every mountain shall be laid low, every valley lifted up. Dr. King used to quote it all the time," Miz Whisnant said and nodded.

"But why you, baby?" Mary sniffed and wiped her eyes.

"Mama, please don't cry," Lisa begged, but showed no sign that she was about to break emotionally. "It's like Jesus said about the wind, Mama. We can't control it."

"A very unusual child," W. Dixon mused.

"So it is not an impossible dream?" Carol Tanic asked nobody in particular as she thought about nearly 60 years of wondering why people just hadn't figured out some way to make it be about everybody, about the whole world, about food and peace and medicine and schools.

"No, Ms. Tanic, it is not impossible. In fact, Rudy Dudley believes you people can make it happen. He is quite sure it is not impossible," Lisa said.

"When did he come here?" Mary asked, still sniffing and wiping her eyes.

"Just before you bought the planter, Mama," Lisa said.

"And why didn't Daddy or I see him?" she spoke with a tear soaked voice, knowing pretty well what the answer would be.

"In some ways, for the same reason you never see the angels," Lisa explained patiently.

"Angels?" Miz Whisnant asked.

"She sees angels," Billy Ray mumbled.

"Well land sake, child, you are a special little girl. I used to see them when I was your age, too," Miz Whisnant almost purred with admiration and delight.

"You did?" W. Dixon asked not losing his Jimmy Carter grin.

"I suspect you've seen a few yourself, preacher," Miz Whisnant looked over her glasses at the old TV evangelist.

"Sometimes they are thick as flies," W. Dixon kept grinning and swept his hand in front of his face as though he were waving off flies.

"Lisa, he told you he's been working on this for more than 20 years?" Carol Tanic asked. "Can you tell us more about that?"

"He knows all 26,000 people. He's read newspaper articles about charities, concerts, protests, anything people were doing to help out other people and to create social change. He then cross-referenced the files at Consistent Life and found people he believes are the most caring and socially minded. He then narrowed it to a geographic region where you could pretty easily get in touch with each other and find ways to work together," Lisa said.

Mary got up from her seat and walked back to the coffee pot where another round was running through. She looked at the black stream of coffee running into the pot below.

"We aren't customers of Consistent Life," Mary said. "How did he find us?" She wasn't sure she wanted to hear the answer.

"That's part of what you will find hard to believe," Lisa said.

"Give us a try, child," Miz Whisnant urged.

"Don't tell me he's an angel," Billy Ray grumbled.

"No," Lisa said and shook her head, "but sometimes he acts like one."

When the Cherokee nation was put on a forced march from Western North Carolina to Oklahoma in 1835, another tragedy of U.S. Government policy, not unlike the Iraq war, a percentage of the tribe stayed behind. Many of them hid in the mountain coves and caves and undergrowth of laurel and rhododendron. Some of them stifled cries as they could see from mountain perches their children or parents or brothers or sisters or friends being marched at gunpoint out of a land they had hunted and fished and recorded in their own written language for thousands of years. Their grief penetrated their hearts and muscles like a deep fever and shook them to their cores. They eventually gained recognition by the U.S. Government as the Eastern Band of the Cherokee.

But not all of those who remained behind as the U.S. Army marched them out of the hills had hid among the coves and caves and perched high up to watch and stifle their cries of grief. Some turned themselves into bear and deer and foxes and lived out their days along the streams and rivers of that mountain region. And one turned himself into a hawk and flew high over the torturous trail of tears that led from North Carolina to Oklahoma. His cries were so harsh and haunting that the soldiers would often take aim and fire off a round in his direction. They were amazed at their inability to hit him. Many times after the report of their rifles boomed across the countryside, they were amazed not only that they had missed, but that apparently the hawk had disappeared, only to come back a few hours later and screech and scream into their ears again.

"He's a shape shifter," Lisa said and pulled her lips back in a grimace as she waited for the reaction she feared.

"Oh, no," W. Dixon groaned.

"What's wrong, preacher?" Billy Ray asked.

"They're demons," W. Dixon lost his grin and pursed his mouth and began glancing around the room nervously. "This is spiritual warfare."

"Oh, come on," Carol Tanic objected and opened her hands to signal her disbelief in W. Dixon's sudden change of mood.

"He's not a demon," Lisa spoke softly, but firmly.

"You don't know, Lisa," Billy Ray scolded.

"Daddy," Lisa objected without whining. "I do know. I know about these things."

"Billy Ray, do not attack our daughter," Mary retorted, still holding her spot by the coffee pot.

"I'm sorry," W. Dixon stood and looked around at the others. "I have to pray about this. Please excuse me."

"Preacher, you're being unfair," Carol objected.

"It certainly feels that way to me, Rev. Franklin," Miz Whisnant chimed in.

"I don't take my spiritual guidance from women," Franklin murmured and waved his hand. "I don't mean anything personal by that." He started walking out of the room.

"It's hard for me not to take it personally, sir," Carol bristled.

"Lord help us," Miz Whisnant groaned, but nothing would stop W. Dixon. He practically bolted through the front door.

"I knew it. I just knew it would come to something demonic," Billy Ray looked around to see he was suddenly surrounded by three grown women and his daughter. "It goes all the way back to Eve in the garden of Eden tempting Adam."

"Daddy," Lisa said in a barely audible voice and reached to touch his arm.

"Honey, I'm sorry, but I've got to get some fresh air and think about this. This is starting to feel like witchcraft to me," Billy Ray stood.

"Billy Ray, sit down," Mary took a step toward him, and his eyes opened like saucers. He froze for a second and eased back into his kitchen chair. "There was a Shoshone medicine man named Rolling Thunder. I've read a couple of books about him. He used to stop his students or people he was treating. He would say at some critical moment, 'Whatever you say right now is how it's going to be.' Now, Billy Ray Crenshaw you are at one of those moments. You walk out of this kitchen with your daughter pouring her heart out, with these good friends bringing all they can to help us figure out what in blue blazes is going on here, and you might as well keep on walking, because we need you as much right now as we have ever needed you."

Billy Ray looked at a woman he had trusted with the deepest longings of his life, and knew she was making more sense than anybody else right that second.

"Could I have another cup of coffee?" he asked and smiled.

"Good answer," Mary said. "Now, where were we?"

"Lisa was telling us that Rudy Dudley is a shape shifter," Carol said.

"And a great man of love," Lisa added. "He believes love is harder than shape shifting. I was amazed that he could do it. He showed me his power to shift the night he came here, but then he told me it's harder to love."

Silence fell in among them for a moment. Billy Ray reached across the kitchen table and touched his daughter's arm.

"I love you, Lisa," Billy Ray said.

"Another good answer," Mary said.

"I love you, Daddy, and I hope you can understand that Mr. Rudy Dudley would never hurt a fly. He's just too tender hearted, but he told me there are so many hurt people in the world who keep hurting other people that it is going to be very hard, very hard to teach love to end all that hurting, to bring people together."

"That makes good sense, honey. It really does to me, Lisa," Billy Ray said, and blinked back his own tears. He knew W. Dixon Franklin was a powerful man with a lot of fear right that moment, but he also knew if a fight was coming, he would take his daughter's side.

Carol Tanic's heart sank in her chest as she saw this man offering such love to his daughter. It made her miss her son very much.

More silence.

"I'm not sure where we go from here," Abigail Whisnant rumbled with her sweet schoolteacher voice.

"I'm almost scared to say this," Carol Tanic offered. "Maybe we learn more about love. I mean if it really is harder than shape shifting, maybe it's the skill we need."

"We've just seen this little girl and her daddy do some pretty powerful loving, eh?" the old teacher asked.

"Yes," the advertising sales lady agreed and met the teacher's eyes.

"Carol Tanic, I believe I can say that I love you based on our work together so far, the time we have spent sharing meals and organizing meetings. I think I have known you long enough to love you," she spoke so softly and quietly and took Carol's hand and squeezed it.

"And I love you, Abigail Whisnant, for all you have just said and maybe for all that is to come," Carol returned the squeeze and felt her hurt swelling with joy.

"And I love both of you for loving people you've never laid eyes on," Mary said.

"Ya'll ain't going gay on me, are you?" Billy Ray teased and grinned.

"And I love you, Billy Ray Crenshaw," Mary spoke again, "for staying in this room just now."

"Oh, me, too," Carol chimed in.

"It's not easy," he confessed. "Can any of you consider the possibility that this is witchcraft?"

"In the first place, most of us have no idea what witchcraft is. Hollywood and the church have mostly demonized it, although we occasionally get a good witch, like Glenda in 'The Wizard of Oz,'" Carol began.

"No time now for Witchcraft 101, Carol," Miz Whisnant cut her off. "For me, this is not the issue, Billy Ray. Your daughter is a highly gifted spiritual person. Some deep wisdom is being conveyed to her through this experience. We don't have to categorize it for now. A movement has been born around this planter and apparently we are going to learn a lot about love along the way. For now, let's keep life as normal as we can for Lisa, provide her with all the privacy she and you need, and remain open to making the most out of whatever happens next."

"To that end, I'd appreciate you folks letting my highly talented spiritual daughter get to her school books. Home schooling does provide for a little flexibility, but we do have a schedule, and this morning we are a little behind," Mary began to clear coffee cups, and Miz Whisnant and Carol stood on cue.

"So is it witchcraft or not?" Billy Ray wanted to know.

"At the moment, we are studying that question," Miz Whisnant smiled, hugged everyone in the room and left with Carol also hugging and saying her good-byes.

It didn't take much study for W. Dixon Franklin. He prayed for about an hour, talked by phone with a couple of his Bible study mates, and began working on the message he would give his television audience that evening on the local religious channel. He would not be talking about love.

He felt a great sadness come over him, as he realized how unloving his message would have to be.

The flight back to Charlotte felt so strange to Lumkin. He kept running that hospital room scene through his head. What had Merrimon meant about death being no big deal, but life . . . what had he said? Don't blow this, Lumkin. He could remember that, but don't blow what? Listen to that little girl. He remembered that, and Merrimon had made it clear he meant that strange little Crenshaw girl.

And then he remembered his look at the planter. Gracious, what had that been all about? How could his just looking at something so ordinary fill him with a sense of his suddenly being more capable and more joyous, or filling him with a sense that if he did more generous things, he would become even more joyous.

The stranger sitting next to him on the flight spoke.

"You seem to have a lot on your mind," the stranger said.

"You're very perceptive," Lumkin responded and wondered why he would engage a stranger in conversation, but there were lots of new experiences coming his way.

"Mind if I ask what's up?" the stranger asked.

"I'd hardly know how to begin," Lumkin admitted.

"How about just pick a spot and start there?" the stranger asked.

"Have you heard of that planter in the mountains of North Carolina that is drawing people who claim some kind of mystical experience with it?" Lumkin asked.

"I have," the stranger said and nodded.

"Well, it is connected somehow to the insurance company I work for," Lumkin said.

"Refund checks were issued to people who have been visiting the planter and then moving on to create groups that are working on social justice issues," the stranger said.

"You've been following the story quite closely I see," Lumkin turned to look at the man more closely. He looked to be in his mid-thirties, but could have been a little older. He had the jet black hair and ruddy complexion of many Native Americans.

"I'm Rudy Dudley, Mr. Lumkin. Listen to the little Crenshaw girl," he said, stood from his seat, and started down the aisle toward the back of the plane. By the time Lumkin could scramble after him, he was gone. He called for a flight attendant and asked her the name of the man sitting next to him and where he had gone.

"That seat's empty, sir," the flight attendant explained.

Lumkin swallowed hard, looked up at the young attendant, and thanked him. He took a deep breath and tried to stop himself from shaking. Somehow, Merrimon's words came back to him. Dying's no big deal. It's life. Don't screw this up, Lumkin.

W. Dixon Franklin questioned himself again. Maybe the little girl had just had a dream about a shape shifter. But something gripped his imagination. Obviously something powerful was at work in the planter. If it was blessed of God, God would stop him from calling it into question. If God had his divine and unshakable hand on it, nothing W. Dixon Franklin could say or do would affect it. He was certain. The little girl was under the influence of a shape shifter, and that meant heathen, anti-Christian theology. It was all coming clear to him. That Buddhist was in cahoots with demonic powers as well. That Tanic woman was so cocky, and wasn't she divorced and had taken the robes of a minister once? Feminist, Buddhist, shape-shifting, none of it had the mark of Christ upon it. How had he let it go this far? It was time to act.

Carol had the rest of the day off so she drove the half-hour to Mac's cabin and found him getting ready to walk his cat through the woods.

She had no idea how to bring him up to date, so she decided just to walk with him quietly in the woods. They moved among the trees and felt the sunlight play in and out of the branches. Winter was not far off, but like so many autumn days in the mountains, the warm sunlight kept the illusion of eternal warmth on their faces and arms.

Birds chirped. Water played rippling over rocks. The trees held their ground.

"So much energy here," she finally said after they had walked for over an hour. Mac nodded.

Russell Cambry did not return from the Charlotte airport to the Crenshaw home, but rather to his own home, south of Rutherfordton, twenty acres and a big goldfish pond, a wood-working shop, and a woman who loved him.

"Hey, sweetheart," he spoke softly as he padded from the garage into the kitchen.

Tina Cambry looked up from a painting she worked on just beyond the kitchen on their sun porch.

"Hey yourself, Mr. Save The World. How's it going?" she teased playfully. She wore a straight, sleeveless brown shift, and had her white hair pulled back with a tie. He loved her simple, unassuming comfort in the world.

"I think your painting saves the world as much as that planter is going to. If you'd ever spend time with it, I think it would communicate to you how wonderful it is that you paint," he said. He sat in the den at his computer where he could still talk with her and check his email.

"I've looked at it online. It does speak, although I'll be damned if I can figure how," she said. She had grown up Catholic, and much like his Methodist upbringing, it failed to stick. When she used a phrase like, "I'll be damned," the damnation preached by the Catholic church was the furthest thing from her mind. "How many hits have you had?"

"Let me look," he said and clicked over to planterspiritwork.org, the domain name he had purchased to keep live images of the planter available worldwide through a web cam. "Still less than a hundred thousand. We aren't exactly the web site de jour."

He stared at the image for a few seconds and felt again the certainty that he could do amazing and heroic things, that his work would matter in the widest scheme of ending war and feeding the world. He had to admit the feeling made no sense, but he felt righteously heroic. It felt great.

He saw something strange. One of the leaves on one of the ivy vines cascading off the rim of the planter disappeared. It was a leaf right at the edge of the top. It was a leaf that was outlined by the blue siding on the Crenshaw's double-wide. It was there as Russell looked at it, and it disappeared.

He picked up his land line, dialed the security company that he had hired to patrol the property, and asked for Billy Smith.

After a quick exchange of pleasantries, he asked, "Billy, I need the video from the last five minutes on the web cam. Yes, the one on the planter itself. Right. Last five minutes as quickly as you can grab it. Thank you."

The web cam and other security cameras on the property digitally recorded on a four-day loop, so tons of video was available, but Russell just needed those last five minutes.

The email arrived in his inbox.

He played it. No question. The leaf disappeared.

"Tina, could you come here a minute?" he asked.

She put down her paintbrush, walked to her husband, rested her hands on his shoulders and squeezed gently.

"Watch this," Russell said. He clicked on the video. "Watch that leaf right there."

"Huh?" Tina asked. "Play it back again."

He did.

"It's got to be some kind of skip in the recording. Maybe the wind blew it off and the camera just missed the wind hitting it."

"It's real time. Look up in the corner. The clock runs in hundredths of a second. There's no skip in the recording. Watch it again."

They watched it four more times.

"The leaf is there one second and gone the next," Tina said.

"It sure looks that way to me. I think the girl knows what's going on. She was just about to tell a bunch of stuff when I had to take Lumkin back to the airport. I asked Carol Tanic to call me, but she hasn't. I've got to get back over there and find out what's going on."

"Sweetheart, don't go over there just now. I miss you so badly when you're away," she said and massaged his shoulders a little more deeply.

"Really?" he turned to face her, and she bit her bottom lip and nodded. "Well, I guess I could hang out for a while."

"I would like that so much," she said and smiled.

Abigail Whisnant sat in the living room of her Polkville home and clicked through web sites that referred to shape shifters. She found nothing surprising. Mythological characters from native and other cultures, like fairies and gnomes, their legend predated history, but also there was no physical or scientific evidence they ever walked among people like rabbits or squirrels or lions or tigers or bears.

She got up, fixed herself a cup of tea, and wondered for the thousandth time where all this was going. She worried about the witchcraft accusations from Billy Ray and felt some fear at the remarkable shift in Rev. Franklin. She considered sending emails to leaders among the people who had been attending meetings and warn them of possible trouble out of Franklin, but thought better of it. She knew in her heart there was no devil in that little girl and that planter, so she decided to wait and see on Franklin's next move.

"That little girl and that planter?" she said aloud. "Why did I put it that way? Hasn't it always been about the planter? Why now does it feel like the little girl is so critical to everything that is happening?"

Rev. Franklin thought about the times in his life people had told him, "You don't have a mean bone in your body." He looked in the mirror at the television station one more time before walking in front of the camera. He prayed one more time, "Not thy will, but mine be done."

He spoke words that made him sad and afraid for the future, "Friends, you know I have always stressed the love of Christ in my Bible teaching here on this program. I truly believe the Bible when it says grace is sufficient to meet every need. But sometimes we have to be inspectors of fruit, as our Lord told us, and I am afraid and deeply saddened to think that many of our neighbors, including myself up to this point, have been fooled by some bad fruit."

He paused, looked away from the camera, sipped from a glass of water, and looked back into the camera.

"As many of you know, there is a planter sitting on the deck of a nice young couple outside of Rutherfordton. The planter gives people a sense of personal power, and I believed initially that it was a good thing, but I have come to my senses. I have prayed about this, and I believe anyone who feels euphoria or ecstasy in the presence of this planter is in fact being influenced by a demonic spirit, and I disavow any support I have given to people visiting that planter or anything I might have said that would have made people think it is a miracle of God. I'm convinced it is demonic and should be shunned."

Rev. Franklin basically harped on that theme the next 29 minutes. His normal half hour of Bible teaching has been preempted by the scare Lisa Crenshaw threw on him by calling the software engineer a shape shifter. He talked about Native American shape shifters, medicine men, ghost shirts, and other traditions of Native spirituality about which he knew little, but he knew enough to feel threatened.

Normally, the broadcast was seen by a few thousand folks in the immediate vicinity, and that would have been that, but a young, ambitious engineer in the station had a buddy who worked at Fox News. He emailed the broadcast to Fox and within hours, America's fairest and most impartial news network was on the phone to Rev. Franklin asking for an interview.

Jenifer Davis felt vindicated and horrified in the same breath. A story she felt should have been national and sensational became one, but not in the way she had hoped and not for the reasons she had hoped. She thought the story was that the planter gave a few hundred people hope of doing great good, enough good to begin organizing and working on social justice issues. Fox News had found a Bible teacher wiling to accuse a local family of being possessed by a demon. Jenifer mused in her heart that somehow that was an altogether different story.

She made a few phone calls, including one to the Crenshaw home, typed up her story for the The Daily Courier, and climbed in her car to drive up and take pictures of TV vans parked on Brown Mountain Road, hoping to get videotape of a demon.

"I believe you know a little about the news business," she said to Miz Whisnant as the two women looked out on the carnival show that had once been a fairly peaceful hillside.

"You mean how Bull Conner was such a big help to Dr. King by sending dogs and men with billy clubs on horseback to attack us?" Miz Whisnant asked.

"Yeah, something like that," Jenifer replied with a smile.

"News folks love a good guy and a bad guy. Looks like Rev. Dixon has decided to make this whole thing about good and evil," the retired schoolteacher shook her head and clucked her tongue in disbelief.

"But isn't that what it is about?" Jenifer asked.

"Can't be just that, child. There were plenty of bad guys in Dr. King's organization and the man himself made many a mistake. There were some good guys among Bull Conner's forces, people who thought they were doing the right thing, anyway. Rarely ever is there pure good on one side and pure evil on the other. We're all human," she intoned with the deliberation of the preachers she had been listening to for more than 70 years. Jenifer had the good sense to wait for her to go on. "This story is about what people think they can do. My mama didn't want me to march with Dr. King. I'd call her from somewhere on the road and she would beg me to come home. 'You can't win, Abigail. White folks ain't gonna give up their way of life,' she would beg and cry and break my heart. But Dr. King had all of us believing God was on our side; and we won. We didn't win it all, and God knows the struggle is still going on. But we can eat in any restaurant in the country now and stay in any motel and sit wherever we want in a movie house or on a university campus. That makes a world of difference, Miss Jenifer. Oh yes, that makes a world of difference."

Jenifer scribbled in her notebook and looked up to see the old teacher smiling at her.

"You gonna put all that in the newspaper instead of writing about all these TV trucks?" Miz Whisnant asked.

"I just want to make sure I get the story right, ma'am," Jenifer said.

Inside the Crenshaw home, Russell Cambry and Lumkin sat across from each other.

"He is a leaf on that vine," Lisa Crenshaw said from a seat beside the same table with the two grown ups on either side of her.

"And sometimes he is not a leaf on that vine," Cambry offered unfolding his hands like he might be a salesman making a presentation.

"That's right," Lisa agreed.

"And sometimes he pops onto airplanes flying 600 miles per hour at 35,000 feet in the air," Lumkin said. He had just told Lisa and Cambry his story of meeting the shape shifter on his flight back from Omaha.

"So, I guess you understand now why your boss told you not to arrest him. No prison can hold him," Lisa said.

"My boss died this morning," Lumkin said and shook his head in disbelief. "I have a hard time imagining our company without Mr. Merrimon. He had been there for such a long time."

"Maybe where he is going he will decide to stay much longer," Lisa said and smiled.

The two grown men laughed.

"He told me I should listen to you, Lisa," Lumkin said. "What do you have to say to me?"

"Well, nothing much. You've already given Mr. Cambry the list of 26,000 names. He'll be using that list to go on with the organizing and the meetings and the dreams of helping everybody work together to benefit everybody. I guess it's all pretty simple from here on out."

"Oh, how I wish I could believe that," Cambry said and chuckled softly.

"Your not believing it will only slow things down," Lisa reminded him.

"But what do you have to say to me, Lisa? Mr. Merrimon was quite convinced you have special gifts and that your message to me would be very, very important," Lumkin begged.

Lisa twisted her little freckled face to one side. She looked up into the corner of the room.

"Tell me what Mr. Merrimon said to you," Lisa asked.

"He said dying is no big deal. But life, something like that, life is what really matters. He said 'Don't blow it, Lumkin.'"

"Good advice, don't you think?" Lisa asked.

"Well, I don't know what it means," Lumkin admitted.

"It means a million different things whatever people might hear it. It means follow your dreams and follow you heart and be careful to not to hurt other people and live life with joy and freedom. Does any of that make any sense?" the little girl asked.

"I'm not sure I have a heart or dreams," Lumkin said.

"Did you always want to be an accountant for an insurance company?" Lisa asked.

"I always wanted to be safe and secure, to not bother anybody and not wear clothes or eat foods or do things that drew any attention to myself," Lumkin said.

"Are you married?" Lisa asked.

"I was, but she became exasperated with me and ran off with a circus clown," he said.

"Did you go after her? Did you try to win her back?" Lisa asked.

Lumkin dropped his head and barely muttered, "No."

"Did you love her?"

"I think I did. It hurt me terribly to lose her. I still keep her picture by my bed. I look at it often and long for her," Lumkin said.

"Oh, my," Russell groaned thinking of his own wife and how good it had felt to be loved by her.

"Go find her," Lisa said.

"What?" Lumkin replied in disbelief.

"She's tired of the clown by now. Clowns can be exasperating, too. If you go find her, it will melt her heart like snow in sunlight. Go find her," Lisa said.

"But I'm not sure I can," Lumkin protested.

"On his death bed, Mr. Merrimon told you to listen to me. I'm telling you to go find her," Lisa said.

"But . . ." Lumkin stammered.

"What's her name?" Lisa asked.

"Wilhemina," the accountant said as if her were saying the sweetest word he had ever spoken.

"Go find Wilhemina," Lisa said, "and tell her you love her with all your heart."

Lumkin looked down at his hands folded on the kitchen table. He looked back up at Lisa and Cambry. "Okay, I will," he said, stood, said his good-byes and left.

"Are you sure about that?" Cambry asked.

"I don't know," Lisa said and shook her head. "A man who's afraid he has no heart and no dream needs something to chase. Maybe she is exasperated with the clown by now. Maybe she can bring him to life."

"You are a very unusual little girl," he said.

"I have a lot of strange friends," she said and smiled. He threw his head back and laughed very loudly.

Mary Crenshaw's face flashed on millions of television sets.

"No, my planter is not demonically possessed. It does seem to have the effect on people of making them want to be nice to other people. Wouldn't that be a strange thing for a demon to do?" she said.

The web site was swamped. Cambry had gone to work quickly to make sure it did not shut down. Software engineers worked like bees to keep it up as millions logged on to view the planter from the web camera. Hundreds of cars clogged the roads into Brown Mountain Road, and the sheriff and highway patrol went to work diverting traffic. Brown Mountain Road had to be closed, and the TV trucks were asked to go home, too. Reporters shouted at sheriff's deputies and lawsuits were filed, but the Crenshaw home was private property, and the law officers had the right to keep the roads open.

Cambry met with Lisa, Billy Ray, and Mary, Mz. Whisnant and Carol Tanic, a few other leaders from the various support groups.

"We have to move it," Cambry said. "It is now touching more lives than this hillside can handle."

"Why not just store it somewhere out of sight?" Billy Ray offered.

An awkward silence followed.

"Can't do that, Daddy," Lisa said and winked at her befuddled father.

"Well, it belongs to us. I reckon we can do anything we want to with it, can't we?" Billy Ray asked and looked around at people he had not known just a few weeks earlier.

"I reckon it doesn't belong to us anymore, Billy Ray," Mary said softly, working to understate that which to her and Lisa had become pretty obvious. "The planter belongs to the whole world now, sweetheart."

Billy Ray looked into the corner of the room, crossed his arms and sighed. He looked around at the others and nodded his head.

The prime minister of Israel walked out of a cabinet meeting and strolled down the hallway into the office of his press secretary.

"Why are you crying?" the prime minister asked.

"Look at this," the press secretary pointed at his computer screen where the planter was in sharp focus.

After a few seconds, the prime minister uttered, "Oh, my."

Two North Carolina highway patrolmen leaned against the fender of a patrol car and looked across the yard where only hours before a bevy of TV trucks had been crowding each other for space, where now only the friends and family of this strange event were meeting inside the double wide trailer.

"Have you looked at it?" one of the patrolmen asked the other.

The second man only glanced at the first.

"Pretty weird, huh?" the first man asked.

"You see a lot in this business," the second man said.

Both men just shook their heads.

In Kansas, a wheat farmer, who had not spoken to his sister in 30 years, drove the four miles that separated their homes.

He stood on her porch with his cap in his hand for a long time. Finally she glanced through her kitchen window and saw him standing there. She walked out onto the porch and stood about three feet from him. Neither of them spoke. Slowly she opened her arms. He stepped into them.

They held the embrace, each feeling the weight and heat of the other's body for a moment or two or three. She pulled out of the embrace.

"You saw that damn planter on the Internet, didn't you?" she asked.

He nodded and said, "I'm so sorry. I was so stupid."

"Me, too. You still drink coffee?" she asked.

"Is the Pope a Catholic?" he asked.

"Come on. I got a fresh pot," she said, and they walked inside.

Cambry said, "We need a big place, maybe a sports arena."

"But aren't sports arenas used for ballgames and stuff like that?" Lisa asked.

"If it's going to draw thousands of people, and if they're going to come for years and years," Carol Tanic began, but Lisa interrupted her.

"It's not going to be like that," Lisa said. "Mr. Cambry is going to buy an abandoned grocery store in Rutherfordton with a nice big parking lot. You guys will figure out how to remodel it and turn it into a visitor center. A couple of shuttle buses will run eight or ten hours a day. We can put a little gate house on either entrance to Brown Mountain Road and limit traffic to locals and the shuttle buses. We can charge a little for the bus ride to cover costs and make it clear to everybody that no one will be turned down because of an inability to pay."

She paused and looked around at everybody.

"You think you can cover that, Mr. Cambry?" she asked.

"Sounds a lot cheaper than buying a sports arena," he answered and laughed.

Carol Tanic and Abigail Whisnant opened an office in the visitor center working to co-ordinate the meetings of the 26,000 people who had received the refund checks and other folks who began meeting to find out how they could maximize the effects of their good intentions.

Russell Cambry began receiving a small income from the bus rides and donations at the visitors center which defrayed the costs of maintaining the web site.

The Kansas farmer and his sister, who was also a farmer, organized a family reunion where they proposed a co-operative relationship with wheat farmers in West Africa.

Of the 26,000 recipients of refunds checks, 37 launched campaigns for mayor, county commissioner, soil and water conservation district, and congress of the United States.

After a series of meetings with his advisors and leaders of the Knesset, the prime minister of Israel picked up the phone and called the president of the Palestinian Authority. They agreed to meet in three weeks. The prime minister asked the president to please take a look at the planter on the Internet. The president said he already had. The two men were delighted by the sound of each other's laughter over the telephone lines.

Mary and Billy Ray Crenshaw started going to marriage counseling because Billy Ray said he was having a hard time getting used to the idea that women might be the equals of men. Mary had kissed him sweetly and commented, "It's just lovely that you might entertain the thought."

Lisa Crenshaw asked to be enrolled in Pinecrest Elementary School, just a few miles from their home. She started the new year as a sixth grader.

On the first day of school, her teacher introduced her to the class and asked her to say a few words. She stood from her desk and walked to the front of the room.

"I know some of ya'll think I'm a weirdo," she said, and the class exploded with laughter.

"Class," the teacher scolded, but Lisa said, "It's okay, ma'am. I am kind of a weirdo." More laughter, but a little softer this time. The teacher pushed her hand out flat to silence the class.

"But I think I am a good kind of weirdo. I'm a weirdo who has been very, very lucky to have magic in my life, not black magic like some people think it is, but sweet magic, like when some guy pulls a dove out of a hat. Mine may be a little harder to explain, but it seems to me that human beings have always known we could do better than we have done. We've always suspected that war was crazy and stupid and horrible and awful. We've always known there was enough food around to feed everybody. We just needed a little more faith in ourselves to make it happen. Well, I've been lucky enough to be kissed by the angels. That's an old Irish expression to be kissed by the angels, and I've got a lot of Irish in my blood, as I know a lot of you do, too. So I'm looking forward to a nice year. I plan to be nice to all of ya'll and sometime soon, my mama says ya'll can come out to my house and have ice cream and see my planter."

Author's notes

November 14, 2008, an extremely lovely day, driving home from Shelby, glancing over on Marion Street and seeing the planter, knowing then I would write another book.

December 8, 2008—dreamed I was in a huge sports arena alone and over the PA system came, "Preach the Gospel." I figured that was nonnegotiable and had immediate confirmation that it is a thing I can do and do well. Probably means something different to me than it does to other people.

Aug. 6, 2009—This book was written primarily at the home of Thomas McBrayer Hicks, one of my dearest friends and one of the finest men I have ever known, although he shuns such praise because he is so aware of his faults. However between July 2 and today, a period of 36 days, the book has also received tons of attention at The Rebirthing Center in Waynesboro, Va. The Gateway Inn in Virginia Beach (Courtesy of the United States Navy,) 625 Halstead Dr. Charleston, S.C., the incredibly beautiful home of Erin and Ed Kosak, the interior of Gabriele's 1995 Toyota Previa en route from spot to spot, and the home of Andy Buck and Sarai LaRocque in Colorado Springs and the home of Steve Krajacic in Crestone, Colorado. At this moment, Gabriele is calling it a night in the back of the van, and I'm typing in the front seat at a campsite in the Carson National Forest outside of Questa, New Mexico. The trip has been a hoot. She is wonderful.

Halloween, 2009—Finished the first draft, now sending it around for people to read. Love to anybody reading this book.

March 6-7, 2012—Time for the long thank you note. Gabriele Rissmeyer, Kathy, Aaron, and Dan's mama, is my beloved partner, who listened to me read most of this to her for weeks and weeks and again tonight. She has been encouragement and love at a level that would make rocks sing if I failed to sing her praises. She loves rocks. Pete Gaither, Mary Jo Cartledgehayes, Jill McBurney, and Bob Brown all read it and gave me feedback. Pete deserves a special thank you, because she really, really liked it. The nice folks at The Greenville

Unitarian Universalist Fellowship have provided a level of love and friendship and encouragement that is beyond all previous standards. Gary Phillips, Ilana Dubester, Shirley Rawley, Earl Crow, Dottie McIntyre, Martha Birt, Anita Wilkie, and the rest of the family, including so many who crossed over, have given so much, been so encouraging and affectionate. I just love that. Amazing support and friendship have come from Deb and Garry Griffith, Linda Ketner, Harriet and McIver Watson, Elayna Shakur and her family, so many sweet friends at Unity of Charleston, The Unitarian Universalist Congregation of the Low Country, Unity Church of Hilton Head, UU Fellowship of Hendersonville, and kind friends throughout the UUA and all of United Methodism. My children: Pepper, P.J., Jessie, Sarah, Katie, and Luke are such great joys, and I hope they know I feel that way about them. My daughters-in-law, Sarah, Rebecca, and Laurie are fine women and deserve everything good that ever happens to them. My delightful granddaughters, Maggie and AV, could go to college on the money we make off this book. Maybe. Maybe not. I'm grateful in the extreme for the love and encouragement of Mott and Dean Buff, Bunny and Charles Burgin, Mike Thompson, Penn Dameron, Scott Hollified, Mike Jones, Carol Yancey, Linda Whisnant, Elaine Bliss, Elaine and Reagan Clark, Ernie Lewis, Patty Dorian and Eino Lindfors,

Leif Diamant, Kim Taylor, Tommy Hicks (who calls me the best writer in North Carolina) Tim Luckadoo, Gavin Harrimon, David Gillespie, Donna Stroud, Shree Yongue and so many of you. Not everybody is crazy about me. There is a group of people who think I'm lower than snake doody, and they would cringe to see their names in this thank you note. They know who they are. Yet I owe them a great debt, too. Some were kind to me beyond any reasonable expectation and I thank them. Others taught me, fought for me, bought me stuff, and ended up feeling betrayed. I'm mighty sorry about that. Deeply and sincerely sorry.

In the last thank you note I wrote in the back of a book, I said Cookie Washington deserved her own sentence. She told me later, she felt as though it should have been a whole page. While I still can't spare a page, I will give her a paragraph. Through her, I came to know so many friends in Charleston and other places in South Carolina. She has promoted my work, encouraged my writing and singing, and been a friend like few could ever be. How about that, Cookie?